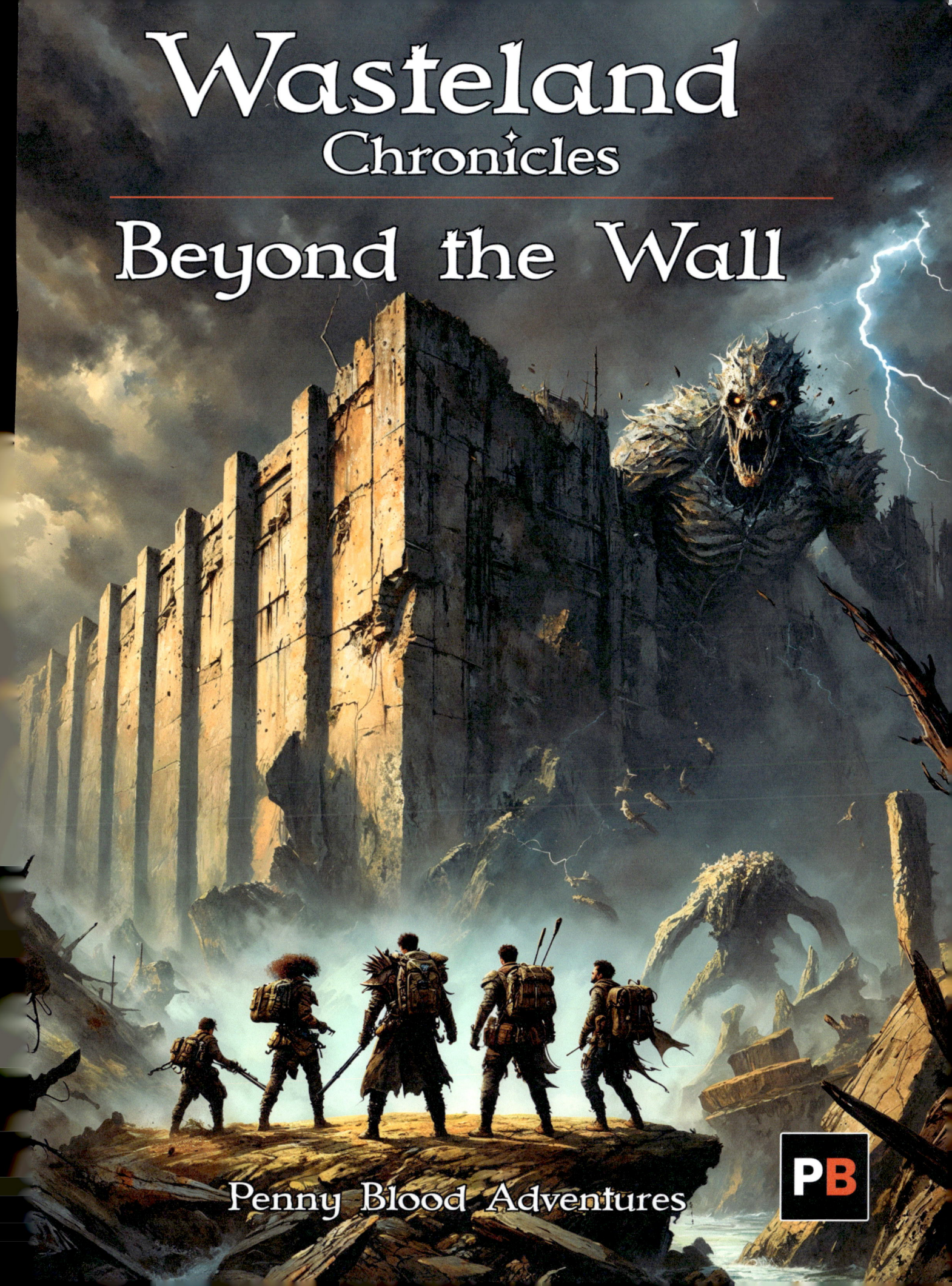

Wasteland Chronicles
Beyond the Wall

Collect All The Penny Blood Adventures

Adventures

- The Dark Nun's Church
- Marie Laveau's Army
- The Werewolves of London
- The Thirteenth Hour
- The Mad Lab
- Krampus
- Midwinter Vampires
- Walk the Plank
- The Leprechaun's Trap
- Mutanti - Whispers of War

- Mutanti - Tears of War
- Mutanti - Lords of War
- The New Dark Age
- Crescent Moon Circus
- Catalyst
- Clockwork Tower
- Gorgon
- The Illustrated Troll
- Witches of the Blood Moon

- The Christmas Chronicles of Winterglen
- The Dragon's Heir
- Pyramids of Power
- Dragon's Rise
- Crypts of the Shadow Court
- Dragon's War
- Battle Cry!
- The Triskelion Prophecy
- Wasteland Chronicles: Beyond The Wall

Compilations

- Gothic Horror - 5 Gothic Horror Themed Adventures
- PBA Vol 1 - 4 Adventures
- The Mutanti Cycle
- The Shattering
- Mysteries of Myth and Machine

Supplemental Rules Books

- Arcane Codex
- Creatures of the Realm
- Gourmet Guildmaster
- Breath of the Dragon
- Stories of the Fey
- Pocket Game Master: Magic Items
- Wasteland Chronicles: The Wasteland

Credits

Author: M A D (aka, Matthew David)

Editor: Alysson Wyatt

Lead Game Testing: Team Wyatt

Game Testers: All of Team Wyatt's friends - you guys rock!

Artists: Adobe Stock Art, Adobe Firefly, Adobe Photoshop, DALL-E, Midjourney

Beyond the Wall

Managing Encounters

Managing Encounters

To help DMs tailor the adventure to the party, each encounter is designed with flexibility in mind. Whether your group consists of fledgling adventurers or seasoned heroes, the provided guidelines will help ensure that the challenges are both fun and fair.

Encounter Structure

Encounter Name: The title of the encounter, usually indicating the primary theme or challenge.

DM Information: A brief summary to give you a clear picture of the encounter's purpose and its role in the overall adventure.

Read Aloud: Descriptive text meant to be read verbatim to the players, setting the scene and atmosphere.

Activity: Detailed guidance, including potential variations, expected player strategies, and potential outcomes.

Lair Actions: Specific actions or effects that occur in certain locations, often benefiting the encounter's primary antagonist.

Scaling the Encounter: Instructions on how to adjust the encounter's difficulty based on player levels:

• **Beginner (Level 1-5)**: Simplified challenges tailored for newer or less powerful characters.

• **Intermediate (Level 6-10)**: Moderate challenges that require a mix of skill, strategy, and teamwork.

• **Advanced (Level 11+)**: Complex and multi-faceted challenges suitable for veteran adventurers.

Monster and/or NPC: Details or references to any creatures or characters the players might interact with during the encounter.

Encounters may reference content found later in the book, such as detailed monster statistics in the Monsters section. Feel free to adapt or replace these elements to better fit your group's preferences or the storyline you're weaving.

Modularity and Flexibility

This adventure, like all Penny Blood Adventures, is modular by design. If a particular monster or challenge doesn't resonate with your campaign's theme, feel free to replace it or adjust as needed. The goal is to provide a rich framework that sparks inspiration, allowing you to craft an unforgettable journey for your players.

Getting Started

Getting Started

The World of *Beyond the Wall*

The Wasteland: Centuries ago, the world was a thriving hub of advanced technology and civilization. Innovations in energy, biotechnology, and artificial intelligence reached unprecedented heights. However, this golden age came to a catastrophic end when a series of technological and environmental disasters struck simultaneously, a result of unchecked experimentation and exploitation of natural resources.

The Catastrophe

Energy Collapse: A revolutionary but unstable energy source, known as Quantum Fusion, was developed to power the world. An unforeseen chain reaction caused a global meltdown of power grids, leading to widespread destruction and chaos.

Biotechnology Gone Wrong: Genetic engineering experiments aimed at enhancing human abilities and agriculture backfired, creating aggressive mutations in both humans and wildlife. These mutations spread rapidly, causing panic and further destabilizing society.

Environmental Havoc: Intensive resource extraction and pollution had already pushed the planet to the brink. The energy collapse and biotechnological failures triggered severe climate changes, resulting in extreme weather patterns, desertification, and the collapse of ecosystems.

The Creation of the Wall

In a desperate bid to contain the chaos, the pre-apocalyptic government embarked on a monumental project: the construction of the Wall. The Wall was designed to serve multiple purposes:

Containment: It was meant to quarantine the areas most affected by the disasters, preventing the spread of mutations and environmental degradation.

Protection: The Wall provided a barrier against the mutated creatures and the hostile climate, offering a semblance of safety to the surviving pockets of civilization.

Separation: The Wall symbolized a final attempt to separate the remnants of organized society from the uncontrollable chaos outside.

Built with advanced technology and reinforced with layers of defenses, the Wall stretched across continents, towering over the landscape as a last bastion of hope.

The Fall into Ignorance

As the years turned into decades and then centuries, the initial knowledge and purpose behind the Wall began to fade. Several factors contributed to this collective amnesia:

Loss of Records: The catastrophic events destroyed many records and knowledge repositories. Libraries, data centers, and archives were lost, and with them, the detailed history of the world before the Wall.

Survival Focus: The immediate need to survive in the harsh new reality shifted focus from preserving history to securing daily necessities. Oral traditions replaced written records, leading to the distortion and loss of detailed information over generations.

Isolation: The communities on either side of the Wall became isolated. With no means to communicate or verify historical facts, myths and legends replaced factual history.

Regimentation and Control: In enclaves like Utopia, militaristic and authoritarian regimes rose to power. These regimes often suppressed historical knowledge to maintain control, promoting a narrative that focused on the present struggle and loyalty to the enclave.

Technological Decline: The advanced technology that built the Wall and society began to deteriorate without proper maintenance. Skills and knowledge needed to operate and understand this technology were lost over generations, further deepening the gap in historical understanding.

Present Day

In the present day, the world is divided into distinct regions, each with its own challenges and characteristics:

The Wasteland: This term encompasses the entire post-apocalyptic world, both inside and outside the Wall. It refers to the harsh, resource-scarce environment that resulted from the Catastrophe. The Wasteland is characterized by extreme weather, mutated wildlife, and the remnants of the old world's technology.

The Walled Territories: These are the areas protected by the Wall, including enclaves like Utopia. While still part of the Wasteland, these regions are considered more "civilized" and offer some protection from the most extreme dangers. Resources are scarce, but there's a semblance of organized society.

Beyond the Wall: This refers to the vast, unexplored, and highly dangerous areas outside the Wall's protection. This is where the players will start their journey. It's considered even more perilous than the Walled Territories, with higher levels of radiation, more aggressive mutants, and lawless regions controlled by raiders and scavengers. Among these rugged regions is the urban ruins of Lost Angeles, where decay has set in and the harsh living of the world "beyond the Wall" has invaded and has reshaped the city.

Hope Falls and Other Outer Enclaves: These are the bastions of surviving humanity outside the protection of the Walled Territories. They represent the last vestiges of organized society, each with its own rules, leadership, and methods of survival.

The Wall itself is viewed differently depending on one's location:

- For those within the Walled Territories, the Wall is seen as an ancient, almost mythical structure of protection. Its origins are shrouded in mystery, and few remember its true purpose.

- For those beyond the Wall, it represents either a barrier to potential resources and safety or a symbol of exclusion and abandonment.

In both regions, the focus is on immediate survival. Resources are scarce, and the environment is hostile. Society has become fragmented, with various enclaves and groups holding onto their own versions of the past, often influenced by superstition and fragmented memories.

The adventure in *The Wasteland Chronicles: Beyond the Wall* offers players the chance to explore both sides of this divided world. As they navigate through the ruins and remnants of the old world, both within and beyond the Wall, they'll uncover fragments of lost history. This journey will lead them to piece together the story of how the Wasteland came to be, why the Wall was built, and ultimately gain a deeper understanding of their world and their place within it.

Objective of the Adventure

The primary objective of *Beyond the Wall* is for the players to venture beyond the Wall to restore the Lifeline Pipeline and secure a stable water source for their enclave, Utopia. The players must navigate through various hazardous environments, encounter mutated creatures, solve ancient puzzles, and confront the remnants of old-world technology. Along the way, they will uncover forgotten histories and face moral dilemmas that will shape the future of their community.

Key Locations and Encounters

Enclave Headquarters

Description: The starting point of the adventure, located within the fortified settlement of Utopia. This area serves as the base of operations for the players, where they receive their mission briefing and gather supplies.

Significance: Players learn about the critical importance of restoring the Lifeline Pipeline and securing a stable water source for Utopia.

NPC: Commander Rylan, who assigns the mission and provides initial resources.

The Wall's Base Camp

Description: A bustling makeshift camp at the base of the Wall, filled with engineers and soldiers working to maintain and monitor the Wall. The camp is alive with activity, but tension runs high due to the looming danger.

Significance: Players receive their final briefing from Engineer Liora and gather essential information and supplies before starting their climb.

NPC: Engineer Liora, who provides technical insight and warns about potential hazards.

The Crumbling Section

Description: A dangerously unstable part of the Wall with large cracks and missing chunks. The air is filled with the sounds of shifting stone and falling debris, making every step a cautious one.

Significance: Players must navigate through this section, avoiding falling debris and structural collapses while dealing with the territorial Dune Drakes.

Encounters: Falling debris traps, Dune Drake attacks.

The Old Security Gate

Description: An ancient, rusted gate embedded in the Wall, with remnants of old-world security systems that can still pose a threat to intruders.

Significance: PCs must disable Security Drones, bypass a laser grid, and solve puzzles to proceed through this section and gain access to a 100-foot tunnel cutting through the Wall.

Encounters: Advanced Security Drones, laser grid, logic puzzles.

The Hidden Armory

Description: A concealed chamber within the Wall, accessible through a hidden entrance obscured by rubble and overgrowth. The Armory contains valuable old-world weapons and gear.

Significance: Players must navigate traps and defeat automated defenses to access the Armory's contents, gaining powerful equipment to aid their mission.

Encounters: Pressure-sensitive floor tiles, complex locking mechanisms, Advanced Security Drones, Techno-Ghosts (which can provide clues about the Lifeline Pipeline and the water source near Hope Falls).

The Lifeline Pipeline

Description: A maze-like network of ancient pipelines that players must navigate to restore functionality. The pipes are filled with echoes of dripping water and the distant hum of old machinery, with some paths leading to dead ends and others stretching on endlessly.

Significance: Players must solve a physical maze puzzle, encounter Toxic Sludges, and consult with Pipemaster Jax to navigate the pipeline and ensure water flows to Utopia.

Encounters: Toxic Sludge monsters, maze navigation, lair actions like corrosive eruptions and structural instability.

NPC: Pipemaster Jax, who offers crucial guidance and knowledge about the pipeline's layout and shortcuts and explains the components necessary to repair the Lifeline Pipeline.

The Dumps

Description: A dense, overgrown forest filled with bizarre, mutated flora and fauna, creating an eerie and dangerous atmosphere. This area is a dumping ground for hazardous waste, leading to its mutated state.

Significance: Players must navigate this treacherous terrain to reach the ruined city, facing numerous environmental challenges.

Encounters: Mutated wildlife (combat encounters), toxic plants (Nature/Survival checks), natural hazards like quicksand or venomous vines.

Lost Angeles

Description: A sprawling urban ruin partially reclaimed by nature, with crumbling buildings and remnants of advanced technology. The city is a dangerous place, inhabited by Scavengers and mutants.

Significance: Players can find clues about the water source here and gather necessary parts to repair the pumps. Lost Angeles is a key location for acquiring old-world technology.

Encounters: Mutated creatures (combat encounters), environmental hazards like collapsing buildings, old-world security systems guarding valuable tech (Technology checks).

NPCs: Scavenger Leader Kael, who controls a faction of Scavengers within the city and can offer information in exchange for assistance.

Hope Falls

Description: A well-hidden, thriving village where a hidden society lives, using a mix of old and new technologies to survive. The village is self-sufficient, with a working water wheel used to generate electricity.

Significance: PCs must gain the trust of the society to access the clean water source and learn about the history of the Wall. Hope Falls is crucial for connecting the pumps and activating the Lifeline Pipeline.

Encounters: Defensive measures set by the hidden society, including traps and guards. PCs may also face challenges in proving their intentions (Persuasion checks).

NPCs: Elder Maren, the wise and cautious leader of the hidden society, who holds vital information and the key to the water source.

Integrating Technology in the Wasteland

In the world of *Beyond the Wall*, remnants of advanced technology play a crucial role. To reflect this, we introduce some new character creation and gameplay features, the Technology skill and engineer's tools. Here's how to incorporate these elements into your game:

Technology Skill: Add Technology as a new Intelligence-based skill. Characters can use this skill for understanding, operating, or repairing old-world tech. When creating characters, allow players to choose Technology as one of their skill proficiencies if it fits their background.

Engineering Tools: Add engineer's tools to the list of available tool proficiencies. These tools are used for more complex technological tasks and repairs. Characters with an appropriate background (e.g., Artificer, Engineer, Tinkerer) can start with this proficiency.

Starting Proficiencies: Characters from tech-savvy backgrounds (determined by the DM) can start with proficiency in the Technology skill and/or engineer's tools. Others can potentially gain these proficiencies through leveling up, choosing them instead of other skills or tools when available.

Gaining Proficiency During Play: Characters can spend downtime to gain proficiency in engineer's tools or the Technology skill. Suggested training time is 10 weeks of downtime, minus a number of weeks equal to the character's Intelligence modifier. Suggested cost for training is 50 gp per week. Alternatively, significant in-game experiences with technology (at the DM's discretion) can grant proficiency.

Using Intelligence (Technology) Skill Checks: Use the Technology skill to identify old-world tech, understand the function of a technological item, or operate unfamiliar devices.

Using Engineer's Tools: Use engineer's tools to repair, modify, or create technological items. DMs can set DCs based on the complexity of a task (e.g., DC 10 for simple devices, DC 20 for complex systems).

Substitutions: If your game doesn't use these new elements or these options don't suit your gaming group, consider substituting Technology skill checks with Investigation or Arcana, and substituting engineer's tools with tinker's tools or a combination of existing tool proficiencies.

Remember, the integration of technology should enhance the post-apocalyptic feel of the setting without overshadowing traditional D&D elements. Use these new mechanics to create unique challenges and opportunities for your players as they explore the remnants of the old world.

Story Hook

The players find themselves in Utopia after receiving an urgent summons from Commander Rylan, the stern and pragmatic leader of the enclave. Each character has a unique reason for answering the call, be it a sense of duty, the promise of rewards, or a personal stake in the mission's success.

You each receive an urgent summons from Commander Rylan, the leader of Utopia. The message, sealed with the insignia of the enclave, reads: "Your skills are needed for a mission of utmost importance. Report to Utopia immediately. Your presence could mean the difference between survival and extinction." Whether driven by a sense of duty, the promise of rewards, or personal motivations, you heed the call and make your way to the fortified walls of Utopia.

Advanced Players

Start the campaign with an encoded message for the PCs. Commander Rylan's message is converted into Morse Code below:

-.-- --- ..- .-. / ... -.- .. .-.. .-.. ... / .- .-. / -. . . -.. . -.. / ..-.
--- .-. / .- / -- .. .. --- -. / --- ..-. / ..- - --- --- ... - / ..
-- .--. --- .-. - .- -. -.-. . .-.-.- / .-. . .--. --- .-. - / - --- / ..- -
--- .--. .. .- / .. -- -- . -.. .. .- - . .-.. -.-- .-.-.- / -.--
--- ..- .-. / .--. .-. . ... . -. -.-. . / -.-. --- ..- .-.. -.. / -- . .- -. / -
- .... . / -.. .. ..-. ..-. . .-. . -. -.-. . / -... . - .-- . .
-. / ... ..- .-. ...- .. ...- .- .-.. / .- -. -.. / . -..- - .. -. -.-. - .. --- -.
.-.-.-

Morse Code is the only method for sending long distance messages in the world of the Wasteland.

GM Tips and Tricks for Running *Beyond the Wall*

Setting the Mood

- Use vivid descriptions to bring the harsh Wasteland to life. Emphasize the desolation, the strange mutations, and the ever-present danger.
- Create a playlist of post-apocalyptic ambient music to enhance the atmosphere during sessions.
- Use props like old, rusted objects or distressed maps to immerse players in the setting.

Managing Complex Scenarios

- Break down complex encounters into manageable parts. For example, repairing the Lifeline Pipeline can be divided into several distinct challenges.
- Use flowcharts or mind maps to keep track of interconnected plot elements and NPC motivations.

- Prepare "story beats" - key points that need to happen - but allow flexibility in how players reach them.

Balancing Survival and Exploration

- Regularly remind players of resource scarcity. Make tracking water, food, and ammunition important.
- Use the environment as a constant antagonist. Radiation zones, toxic areas, and extreme weather can be as threatening as any monster.
- Reward player creativity in using scavenged items or repurposing technology.

Enhancing Player Engagement

- Tie character backstories into the adventure. Perhaps one character has an ancestral connection to Hope Falls or Lost Angeles.
- Offer meaningful choices that impact the story. Decisions about resource allocation or which factions to ally with should have consequences.
- Use the "Flashlight" technique: Give each player a moment to shine based on their character's unique skills or background.

Running Faction Interactions

- Develop distinct personalities and motivations for each faction leader.
- Use a relationship map to track how player actions affect their standing with different groups.
- Allow for complex alliances and betrayals to keep players on their toes.

Managing Technology and Magic

- Treat pre-war technology like magic items. Make them rare, powerful, and often unpredictable.
- Use skill challenges for understanding or repairing advanced tech. This can involve multiple characters working together.
- Be consistent with tech limitations to maintain the post-apocalyptic feel.

Handling Combat in the Wasteland

- Emphasize the deadliness of combat. Encourage players to think tactically and use the environment.
- Use dynamic environments in combat. Collapsing ruins or unstable mutant-infested areas can add excitement.
- Introduce unique Wasteland threats like radiation zones or toxic spores to make combat more than just trading blows.

Encouraging Exploration

- Pepper the Wasteland with intriguing landmarks or mysterious structures to entice players off the beaten path.

- Use rumors and partial information to spark player curiosity about different locations.

- Reward exploration with unique items, information, or allies.

Maintaining Tension

- Use a "Doom Clock" for time-sensitive missions like restoring water flow.

- Introduce complications that force difficult choices. For example, helping one settlement might mean another goes without water.

- Keep a list of random encounters to inject unexpected challenges during lulls.

Adapting to Player Actions

- Be prepared to improvise. Players will often come up with solutions you didn't anticipate.

- Have a list of flexible NPCs, locations, and plot hooks that can be inserted where needed.

- Use player ideas to enhance the story. If they come up with an interesting theory, consider making it true.

Concluding Adventures

- Ensure that player actions have visible impacts on the Wasteland. Show how settlements change based on their decisions.

- Provide epilogues for major NPCs and factions to give closure and set up future adventures.

- End sessions with cliffhangers or new mysteries to maintain excitement for the next game.

Remember, the key to running *Beyond the Wall* is to create a sense of a vast, dangerous, but ultimately survivable Wasteland. Your role is to challenge the players, but also to facilitate their heroic journey in this harsh new world.

Act 1

Act 1 – Facing the Wall

Enclave Headquarters

This is the mission briefing where players learn about the critical need to find water beyond the Wall. They receive their initial resources and assignments from Commander Rylan.

You stand at the heart of a fortified compound, a stark contrast to the desolate wasteland that surrounds it. Makeshift defenses crafted from salvaged materials rise up around you, manned by vigilant soldiers who scrutinize every movement with sharp, alert eyes. The atmosphere is thick with tension, and the echoes of military drills reverberate through the air, underscoring the urgency and discipline that permeates this enclave. The buildings are utilitarian and robust, constructed to withstand both the elements and any potential threats from beyond the Wall.

At the center of this militaristic hub, you are led into a command tent. The heavy fabric walls are adorned with maps and tactical charts detailing the surrounding areas and the Wall itself. A large table dominates the space, covered in documents, plans, and the remnants of hurried meals. The atmosphere inside is one of relentless determination and controlled chaos, a reflection of the dire circumstances that have brought you here. As you take in your surroundings, the weight of your impending mission becomes all the more palpable.

Mission Briefing

Receive your mission details and initial resources from Commander Rylan. Understand the urgency of crossing the Wall and finding water within days to save your homeland.

- This is a critical narrative moment to set the tone and urgency of the adventure.

- Ensure Commander Rylan's stern and authoritative demeanor is conveyed.

- The players should feel the weight of the mission's importance and the dire situation their homeland faces.

Commander Rylan's Speech: *"Adventurers, we are on the brink of collapse. Our water reserves are nearly depleted, and without a new source, we won't survive beyond the next few weeks. Beyond the Wall lies our only hope, a rumored source of clean water. Your mission is to cross the Wall, navigate the dangers that lie beyond, and secure this water source for our survival. Time is of the essence, and failure is not an option. Prepare yourselves, for you venture into unknown and perilous lands."*

Initial Resources

Supplies Provided:

Rations: 5 days of food per character.

Water Skins: Enough to hold 3 days' worth of water per character.

Healing Potions: 2 standard healing potions per character.

Climbing Gear: Ropes, grappling hooks, and other equipment needed to scale the Wall.

Equipment Options: The characters can request specific weapons or armor upgrades if available in the enclave's stores. Roll a d20 to determine availability (DC 12 for standard items, DC 18 for rare items). The PCs will need to take a trip to the Resource Depot to pick out their items.

Skill Challenges

Insight Check (DC 15):

- To gauge Commander Rylan's sincerity and the true urgency of the mission.

- Success reveals that the situation is even more desperate than initially presented. It is suspected that the available water will only last 7-10 days.

Persuasion Check (DC 18):

To request additional resources or more detailed information about the mission.

Success grants one additional piece of useful equipment or a piece of crucial intel about the Wall's defenses or the terrain beyond. Pieces of known information include:

- One section of the Wall is crumbling and may offer a shortcut over the Wall.

- Ancient security systems are known to be in place but may or may not be operational.

- There is rumor of a hidden armory somewhere on or around the Wall.

Interaction with Commander Rylan

Commander Rylan's Responses:

To Requests for More Information: *"We have limited intel on what lies beyond the Wall. What we do know is fragmented and often conflicting. Your best bet is to stay alert and trust your instincts."*

To Concerns About Dangers: *"The dangers are real, but so is our resolve. We've survived this long by facing the impossible. Trust in your training and each other."*

To Requests for Additional Equipment: *"Our resources are stretched thin, but I'll see what we can spare. Every bit of gear you take means less for those*

defending our home. You can meet with the quartermaster at our Resource Depot."

Next Steps

Explore Utopia: Utopia is a small community split into a series of Nissen huts and tents. The people of the community sense that they are near the end of their resources, particularly water. Anxiety is high. As you explore, you learn that Utopia is not alone in its struggles:

- All communities within a vast area are facing severe water shortages due to prolonged drought and environmental degradation.

- Some residents have already left, seeking rumored oases or distant settlements, but the few who returned found nothing.

- The majority of Utopia's population refuses to leave, citing dangers of the Wasteland, loyalty to their home, and skepticism about better conditions elsewhere.

- Reports from traders and scouts indicate that other settlements are equally desperate, making migration a risky gamble.

- Utopia's location near the Wall offers a strategic advantage and relative safety that many are reluctant to abandon.

Commander Rylan and other leaders believe that restoring the Lifeline Pipeline is not just about saving Utopia, but potentially revitalizing the entire region. This mission is seen as a last, crucial effort to avoid a mass exodus into the dangerous unknown.

Visit the Quartermaster: Visit Quartermaster Tags at the Resource Depot and see if there are other items you can take on your journey. Tags can provide more context about the scarcity of supplies and the challenges faced by those who've attempted to find water elsewhere.

Begin Your Journey: Rylan escorts you to the secured gate where you leave Utopia and head towards the Base Camp stationed just in front of the Wall. As you depart, you see the mixture of hope and desperation on the faces of Utopia's residents, underscoring the importance of your mission.

Terrain

The terrain within the Enclave Headquarters is well-organized but cluttered with makeshift defenses and military equipment. Navigating through this area requires careful movement to avoid tripping over supplies or interfering with ongoing drills.

Obstacles: Characters moving at normal speed must make a DC 10 Dexterity (Athletics or Acrobatics) check to avoid tripping over obstacles. Failure results in movement being halved for that turn.

Defensive Structures: Areas around fortified positions provide half cover (+2 to AC and Dexterity saving throws) for those utilizing them.

Lair Actions

On initiative count 20 (losing initiative ties), Commander Rylan invokes one of the following lair actions:

Coordinated Defense: Commander Rylan can order a coordinated defense, granting all soldiers within the enclave advantage on their next attack roll until the start of the next round.

Reinforcement Call: Commander Rylan can summon additional soldiers to the area. 1d4 soldiers arrive at the start of the next round, ready to assist.

Strategic Maneuver: Commander Rylan can reposition any ally within 30 feet, moving them up to their speed without provoking opportunity attacks.

Scaling the Encounter

Beginning Players (PC levels 1-5)

Mission Briefing:

- Emphasize the urgency and importance of the mission, but keep the dialogue straightforward and clear.

- Provide all essential resources as listed.

Skill Challenges: Lower the DCs for Insight and Persuasion checks to 10 and 13 respectively.

Initial Resources:

- Provide 1 additional healing potion per character.

- Ensure the availability of standard weapons and armor upgrades without the need for a roll.

Terrain: Keep the DC for navigating obstacles at 10 but allow rerolls if players fail.

Lair Actions:

- Limit lair actions to once per encounter.

- Coordinated Defense: Advantage on the next attack roll for one soldier.

- Reinforcement Call: Summon 1 soldier instead of 1d4.

- Strategic Maneuver: Allow repositioning of one ally within 15 feet.

Resource Depot

This encounter involves PCs gathering additional supplies or crucial information for their mission. Potential skirmishes with desperate Survivors of Utopia may arise, testing the PCs' negotiation and combat skills.

Intermediate Players (PC levels 6-10)

Mission Briefing:

- Maintain the standard level of detail and urgency.

- Include all essential resources as listed.

Skill Challenges: Use the standard DCs for Insight and Persuasion checks (15 and 18 respectively).

Initial Resources: Offer standard weapons and armor upgrades with a DC 12 roll, and rare items with a DC 18 roll.

Terrain: Keep the DC for navigating obstacles at 10 but increase the penalty for failure (movement halved for 2 turns).

Lair Actions:

- Coordinated Defense: Advantage on the next attack roll for all soldiers within 30 feet of Commander Rylan.

- Reinforcement Call: Summon 1d4 soldiers.

- Strategic Maneuver: Allow repositioning of one ally within 30 feet.

Advanced Players (PC levels 11+)

Mission Briefing: Increase the complexity of the mission details, including more nuanced threats and potential subplots.

Skill Challenges: Increase the DC for Insight and Persuasion checks to 18 and 20 respectively.

Initial Resources: Offer rare weapons and armor upgrades with a DC 15 roll, and very rare items with a DC 20 roll.

Terrain: Increase the DC for navigating obstacles to 15, with failure resulting in the character being prone.

Lair Actions:

- **Coordinated Defense**: Advantage on the next attack roll for all soldiers within 60 feet of Commander Rylan.

- **Reinforcement Call**: Summon 1d4+2 soldiers.

- **Strategic Maneuver**: Allow repositioning of up to two allies within 30 feet.

NPC

Commander Rylan: The stern and pragmatic leader who provides the players with their mission details and initial resources.

You enter a vast warehouse, its towering shelves filled with crates and containers of vital supplies. The air inside is thick with the scent of dust and oil, and the dim lighting casts long shadows across the room. Soldiers patrol the area, ensuring that everything remains secure. In one corner, a group of workers diligently sort through recent deliveries, their faces marked by the weariness of endless vigilance.

At the center of the warehouse stands a command post, where an imposing figure is busy coordinating the flow of resources. The walls are lined with maps and charts, detailing supply routes and inventory lists. Stacks of crates and barrels form a makeshift fortification around the command post, emphasizing the importance of what lies within. The atmosphere here is one of organized chaos, with everyone fully aware of the critical role these supplies play in their survival.

Activities

Gather Supplies: The PCs must interact with Quartermaster Tags to request and gather the essential supplies and information needed for their journey.

Encounters and Conflict: Survivors who live in Utopia angrily approach the PCs about taking precious reserves.

Gather Supplies

The PCs must interact with Quartermaster Tags to request and gather the essential supplies and information needed for their journey.

- Quartermaster Tags is diligent and efficient, but also wary of depleting resources.
- PCs must convince her of the urgency and necessity of their requests.

- Potential disputes or skirmishes with desperate Survivors of Utopia can arise, creating additional challenges.

Interaction with Quartermaster Tags

Roleplaying Guidance:

- Quartermaster Tags is practical and focused, speaking in a measured and authoritative tone.
- She values clear reasoning and evidence of the PCs' need for supplies.
- She may be willing to provide extra supplies if convinced of the PCs' competence and necessity.

Possible Dialogue Prompts:

- *"State your needs clearly. We can't afford to waste resources."*
- *"Convince me this mission is worth the supplies you're asking for."*
- *"Every item you take is one less for someone else. Make sure it's essential."*

Skill Challenges

Persuasion Check (DC 15):

- To convince Tags to provide extra supplies or more detailed information about the mission.
- Success grants one additional piece of useful equipment or an extra day's rations for the party.

Insight Check (DC 13):

- To gauge Tags' mood and tailor the party's approach accordingly.

- Success provides advantage on the next Charisma-based check with Tags.

Investigation Check (DC 14):

- To examine the available supplies and spot useful items that might not be immediately visible.

- Success reveals a hidden cache of useful supplies (e.g., an extra healing potion, additional arrows, or a set of thieves' tools).

Intimidation Check (DC 17):

- To forcefully demand supplies, potentially at the cost of creating tension with Tags and other Survivors.

- Success provides the requested supplies but may result in a negative reaction from Tags and increased difficulty in future interactions.

Potential Outcomes

Successful Interaction:

- Players receive the supplies they need and possibly additional resources.

- Tags provides crucial information about the journey ahead.

- Positive relationship established with Tags, potentially benefiting future encounters.

Unsuccessful Interaction:

- Players receive limited supplies and basic information.

- Tags remains skeptical or distrustful, affecting future interactions.

- Increased likelihood of disputes or skirmishes with other Survivors.

Possible Supplies

Standard Supplies:

- **Rations:** 5 days of food per character.

- **Water Skins:** Enough to hold 3 days' worth of water per character.

- **Healing Potions:** 2 standard healing potions per character.

- **Maps and Charts:** Detailed maps of the Wall and the known regions beyond it.

- **Climbing Gear:** Ropes, grappling hooks, and other equipment needed to scale the Wall.

Special Equipment (Based on Skill Challenges):

- **Weapons and Armor:** Upgrades or additional items based on availability.

- **Tools and Kits:** Thieves' tools, healer's kits, alchemical supplies, etc.

- **Magic Items:** Rare but possible, such as a single-use scroll or potion (DM's discretion).

Encounters and Conflict

Setup:

- The encounter begins as a group of 3-5 desperate Survivors confronts the PCs, demanding supplies.

- Position the Survivors around the warehouse, using the cluttered terrain for cover and tactical advantage.

Tactics:

- The Survivors will initially use cover provided by crates and barrels, moving in to engage PCs in melee combat.

- They will focus on characters who appear to be carrying the most supplies or seem the weakest.

- The Survivors may attempt to retreat if they lose half their number or if they are clearly outmatched.

Negotiation/Intimidation

Setup:

- The Survivors approach the party with a mix of desperation and aggression, demanding supplies to survive.

- PCs can attempt to negotiate or intimidate the Survivors to resolve the situation peacefully.

Skill Challenges

Negotiation (Persuasion Check (DC 15)):

- To convince the Survivors to stand down and accept an alternative solution, such as sharing supplies or promising future help.

- Success results in the Survivors calming down and accepting a compromise.

- Failure results in the Survivors becoming more aggressive, escalating towards combat.

Possible Dialogue: *"We're starving and out of water! We need those supplies more than you do!"*

Intimidation Check (DC 13):

- To assert dominance and scare the Survivors into backing down.

- Success results in the Survivors retreating, fearing the PCs' strength.

- Failure results in the Survivors calling the PCs' bluff and attacking.

Possible Dialogue: *"We won't back down! We need those supplies!"*

Resolution

Successful Negotiation/Intimidation:

- PCs avoid combat and resolve the conflict peacefully.

- Survivors might provide useful information or become future allies.

Combat Victory:

- PCs defeat the Survivors, securing the supplies.

- Potential for moral consequences and future encounters with more desperate groups.

Terrain

The terrain within the warehouse is cluttered with supplies and equipment, creating a maze-like environment. Narrow aisles between tall shelves can restrict movement, and stacked crates provide both cover and obstacles.

Cluttered Pathways: Moving through the aisles requires a DC 10 Dexterity (Athletics or Acrobatics) check to avoid tripping over supplies. Failure results in movement being halved for that turn.

Cover: Crates and barrels provide half cover (+2 to AC and Dexterity saving throws) or three-quarters cover (+5 to AC and Dexterity saving throws) depending on their size.

Lair Actions

On initiative count 20 (losing initiative ties), the Resource Depot and/or Quartermaster Tags invokes one of the following lair actions:

Lockdown Protocol: Automated security systems activate, causing all exits to lock. Characters must succeed on a DC 15 Intelligence (Investigation) check to find a way to override the system and escape.

Supply Cache: Quartermaster Tags can direct the discovery of a hidden cache of supplies. One PC of her choice can retrieve a healing potion or a piece of adventuring gear worth up to 50 gp.

Reinforcement Call: Quartermaster Tags can call for reinforcements. 1d4 additional Survivors of Utopia arrive to assist her.

Scaling the Encounter

Beginning Players (PC levels 1-5)

- Reduce the number of hostile Survivors and lower their stats.

- Decrease DCs for skill checks by 3-5 points.

- Simplify environmental hazards.

Intermediate Players (PC levels 6-10)

- Use standard encounter setups as described.

- Maintain original DCs for skill checks.

- Standard environmental hazards.

Advanced Players (PC levels 11+)

- Increase the number of hostile Survivors and their stats.

- Raise DCs for skill checks by 2-4 points.

- Increase the complexity and intensity of environmental hazards.

Monster

Survivor of Utopia (3-5)

NPC

Quartermaster Tags: The military leader responsible for resource allocation and providing the PCs with essential supplies for their journey.

Exploring Utopia

Utopia is a small, fortified settlement that serves as a haven for its inhabitants in the harsh Wasteland. The encounter involves exploring the settlement, interacting with its residents, and understanding the challenges they face.

You approach a modest collection of structures, each one showing signs of wear and adaptation. The heart of the settlement is made up of Nissen huts, their curved, corrugated metal roofs reflecting the harsh sunlight. These huts are interspersed with makeshift tents, forming a haphazard yet functional community. A wooden fence, cobbled together from salvaged materials, encircles the entire compound, offering a semblance of security. Guards patrol the perimeter, their watchful eyes scanning the horizon for any sign of danger.

Within the community, the atmosphere is tense. The people of Utopia move about their daily tasks with tired, weary expressions. Children play listlessly near the huts, while adults tend to small, struggling gardens or work on repairs with an air of desperation. Faces are etched with lines of fatigue and anxiety, the stress of dwindling resources evident in every action. The air is filled with the scent of cooking fires, but the portions are meager. Conversations are hushed, and the weight of uncertainty hangs heavy over the settlement.

Interact with the Community

Players can speak with the residents of Utopia to learn about their lives, gather information, and possibly gain assistance or supplies for their journey. All attempts to convince an NPC to join the party require a successful DC 15 Persuasion check.

Name	Backstory	Information	Bonus	Convincing Instructions
Clumsy	Clumsy, ironically named for his incredible dexterity, is a former street performer turned thief. His nimble fingers are now put to use scavenging supplies.	Has encountered small raiding parties that have attempted to breach Utopia's defenses. He can warn about their tactics and the territories they've been spotted in near the enclave.	Clumsy grants the party advantage on Dexterity (Stealth) checks and can disarm traps with advantage.	Persuade Clumsy to join by promising to share any loot found.
Fix	An ingenious mechanic and inventor, Fix has dedicated her life to keeping Utopia's machinery running. She often tinkers with old-world tech salvaged from ruins.	Can explain the basics of quantum fusion and its collapse, as well as the current state of technology in Utopia.	Fix provides the party with a +2 bonus on Intelligence (Technology) checks for devices and machinery commonly found in Utopia. She can repair damaged items of moderate complexity (up to the equivalent of uncommon magic items in terms of technological sophistication). However, her ability to understand or repair highly advanced pre-Catastrophe technology (rare or higher equivalent) is limited.	Persuade Fix to join by offering to bring back any old-world tech found during the quest.
Beak	Beak uses his knowledge of flora and fauna to cultivate scarce crops and identify safe plants for consumption.	Provides insights on the biotechnology failures and the aggressive mutations in wildlife and humans.	Beak grants the party advantage on Wisdom (Survival) checks to find food and water, and identify safe or dangerous plants.	Persuade Beak to join by highlighting the importance of his expertise in finding safe food and water.
Wings	Known for his ability to move swiftly and silently, Wings is a courier who transports messages and small supplies between settlements.	Shares rumors about the various tribes and gangs in the Wasteland, including recent sightings and movements.	Wings grants the party a +5 bonus to movement speed and advantage on Wisdom (Perception) checks to spot distant threats.	Persuade Wings to join by explaining the party's need for speed and stealth.
Gloom	A former historian, Gloom is one of the few who tries to preserve the past through storytelling, though his tales are often dark and somber.	Can recount the history of the Wall, its original purpose, and the myths surrounding its construction and maintenance.	Gloom provides the party with a +2 bonus to Intelligence (History) checks and advantage on Charisma (Performance) checks when telling stories.	Persuade Gloom to join by emphasizing the quest's potential to uncover lost knowledge.
Mask	Mask is a master of disguise and deception, using his talents to infiltrate enemy camps and gather intelligence.	Offers information about the fall into ignorance and the loss of records, emphasizing the shift from history to survival.	Mask grants the party advantage on Charisma (Deception) checks and can use the disguise kit proficiently.	Persuade Mask to join by assuring the need for his skills in infiltration and gathering intelligence.
Ghost	An elusive figure, Ghost is an expert tracker and hunter who prefers solitude. She's often seen only when she wants to be.	Knows secret paths and hidden locations in the Wasteland, useful for avoiding danger and finding resources.	Ghost provides the party with a +2 bonus to Wisdom (Survival) checks related to tracking and advantage on Stealth checks in natural terrain.	Persuade Ghost to join by explaining the need for her tracking skills to navigate the Wasteland.

Name	Description	Information	Benefit	Persuasion
Dust	A grizzled veteran of many battles, Dust serves as a trainer for Utopia's militia. His experience in combat is unmatched.	Can provide tactical advice on fighting the mutated creatures and hostile humans in the Wasteland.	Dust grants the party a +2 bonus to attack rolls against mutated creatures and advantage on Wisdom (Insight) checks to predict enemy tactics.	Persuade Dust to join by emphasizing need for his tactical expertise.
Box	Box, named for his bulky frame and strength, is a builder and protector of Utopia. He constructs and maintains the fortifications.	Shares details about the structural aspects of the Wall and the defenses designed to protect the enclaves.	Box provides the party with a +2 bonus to Strength (Athletics) checks and can help reinforce defenses, granting temporary hit points to PCs equal to 2 + the party's average level.	Persuade Box to join by assuring the importance of his strength and construction skills.
Weeds	A former botanist, Weeds has adapted her skills to grow food in the harsh environment. She is passionate about finding new ways to sustain life.	Provides knowledge about the environmental havoc and its impact on the ecosystem, including which plants are safe to eat.	Weeds grants the party advantage on Nature checks and can create herbal remedies that heal 1d8 hit points.	Persuade Weeds to join by emphasizing the quest's need for her botanical knowledge and healing skills.
Nemo	An enigmatic figure with a mysterious past, Nemo is known for his extensive travels and knowledge of the Wasteland's secrets.	Offers rare insights into old-world technology and hidden relics that might be found beyond the Wall.	Nemo provides the party with a +2 bonus to Intelligence (Arcana) checks and can provide the Help action to identify magical items and artifacts.	Persuade Nemo to join by promising to explore and uncover hidden relics and technology together.
Fluque	A quick-witted trader, Fluque deals in rare goods and information. He is always looking for the next profitable exchange.	Can share rumors about the Catastrophe and the marauding gangs, as well as trade valuable items.	Fluque grants the party a +2 bonus to Charisma (Persuasion) checks and can trade for rare items, reducing their cost by 10%.	Persuade Fluque to join by offering to share valuable finds and trade opportunities from the quest.
Bugs	An expert in entomology, Bugs has found ways to harness the mutated insects of the Wasteland for various uses, including food and defense.	Provides information on the mutations in insects and how they can be used or avoided.	Bugs grants the party advantage on Wisdom (Animal Handling) checks involving insects and can create insect-based tools or weapons.	Persuade Bugs to join by highlighting the need for his expertise in dealing with mutated insects.
Hybrid	A survivor of biotechnological experimentation, Hybrid has both human and animal traits. She uses her abilities to scout and protect Utopia.	Shares firsthand experiences of biotechnology gone wrong and the resulting mutations.	Hybrid provides the party with a +2 bonus to Dexterity (Stealth) checks and can track by scent, giving advantage on Survival checks.	Persuade Hybrid to join by explaining the need for her unique tracking abilities and protection skills.
Pygmy	Small in stature but large in spirit, Pygmy is a skilled gatherer who can find food and water in the most unlikely places.	Knows about the best places to find resources in the Wasteland and shares tips on survival.	Pygmy grants the party a +2 bonus to Wisdom (Survival) checks and can find double the usual amount of food and water.	Persuade Pygmy to join by emphasizing the importance of her gathering skills for the quest's survival.

Note: Only one resident can join the players on their quest. Choose wisely based on the party's needs and the challenges ahead.

Terrain

The terrain within Utopia is a mix of flat, compacted dirt paths and uneven ground with scattered debris. The wooden fence and various structures provide cover and obstacles.

Uneven Ground: Moving quickly through the settlement requires a DC 10 Dexterity (Athletics or Acrobatics) check to avoid tripping over debris. Failure results in movement being halved for that turn.

Cover: The wooden fence and buildings provide half cover (+2 to AC and Dexterity saving throws) or three-quarters cover (+5 to AC and Dexterity saving throws) depending on their size.

Visibility: Guards and patrols have advantage on Perception checks to spot intruders within the settlement.

Lair Actions

On initiative count 20 (losing initiative ties), the community of Utopia invokes one of the following lair actions:

Guard Patrol: A patrol of guards passes by, offering assistance or additional security. One guard can aid an ally, granting advantage on their next roll.

Community Effort: The community bands together to help. One PC can receive a boost, such as a healing herb that restores 1d8 hit points or an improvised tool that provides advantage on a single skill check.

Alarm Call: An alarm is raised if danger is detected. All guards within the settlement become alert and mobilize, providing additional protection and possibly calling for reinforcements.

Scaling the Encounter

Beginning Players (PC levels 1-5)

- Reduce the complexity and severity of interactions.
- Lower DCs for skill checks by 3-5 points.
- Simplify environmental hazards and lair actions.

Intermediate Players (PC levels 6-10)

- Use standard encounter setups as described.
- Maintain original DCs for skill checks.
- Standard environmental hazards and lair actions.

Advanced Players (PC levels 11+)

- Increase the complexity and severity of interactions.
- Raise DCs for skill checks by 2-4 points.
- Increase the intensity of environmental hazards and lair actions.

The Wasteland

The party must navigate a one-day hike across the harsh Wasteland to reach Base Camp at the base of the Wall. Random encounters, including the threat of Mutant Hounds, will challenge the PCs' survival skills.

You step out from the relative safety of Utopia into the unforgiving expanse of the Wasteland. The ground beneath your feet is a cracked and parched earth, bleached white by the relentless sun. Sparse, twisted shrubs dot the landscape, struggling to survive in the arid soil. The air is thick with heat, and waves of it distort the horizon, making distant objects appear to shimmer and dance. There is a haunting stillness, broken only by the occasional gust of wind that carries the scent of dust and decay.

As you journey further, the desolation becomes even more apparent. Rusted remnants of old-world vehicles lie half-buried in the dirt, their metal frames twisted and broken by time. The remains of crumbling structures can be seen in the distance, offering a stark reminder of the civilization that once thrived here. Every step you take feels heavy, the weight of your mission pressing down as you make your way towards the distant silhouette of the Wall. Your senses are on high alert, knowing that dangers could lurk behind any mound of debris or in the shadows of the ruins.

Survive the Journey

Players must navigate the Wasteland, dealing with environmental hazards and random encounters, including attacks from Mutant Hounds.

Random Encounter Table

1d20	Encounter Name	Description
1	Mutant Hound Pack	A pack of 3 Mutant Hounds ambushes the party. Use the Mutant Hound stat block. They have advantage on Stealth checks due to their natural camouflage.
2	Desperate Refugees	A small group of 3-5 desperate refugees from a failed settlement approaches the party. They are starving and dehydrated, begging for supplies. Use the Commoner stat block with reduced hit points (1d8). If denied aid, they may become aggressive out of desperation, forcing a moral dilemma on the PCs.
3	Dust Storm	A severe dust storm hits. PCs must make a DC 14 Constitution saving throw or be blinded for 1d4 rounds and take 2d6 bludgeoning damage.
4	Irradiated Pool	PCs encounter a pool of irradiated water. Each PC must make a DC 12 Constitution saving throw or take 3d6 poison damage and gain one level of exhaustion.
5	Friendly Survivor	The party meets a lone Survivor of Utopia who offers information in exchange for food or water. Use the Survivor of Utopia stat block. He will tell you that there is an armory hidden in the Wall. He has a map that shows you the location.
6	Ancient Trap	PCs stumble upon an old world trap. They must make a DC 15 Dexterity saving throw to avoid taking 4d6 piercing damage from hidden spikes.
7	Hidden Cache	The party finds a hidden cache of supplies. Roll a d6: (1-2) 2 healing potions, (3-4) 50 gp worth of rations, (5-6) a minor magical trinket.
8	Heat Wave	An intense heat wave strikes, and shade is scarce. PCs must make a DC 12 Constitution saving throw or take 1d4 fire damage from severe sunburn and gain one level of exhaustion.
9	Rad Beetles	A swarm of 3 Rad Beetles emerges from the ground. Use the Rad Beetle stat block. They can spray acid as a ranged attack.
10	Sandstorm	A sudden sandstorm engulfs the party. All creatures must succeed on a DC 14 Constitution saving throw or be blinded for 1d4 hours. For the duration of the storm, vision is limited to 10 feet, Perception is rolled at disadvantage, and movement is halved.
11	Dune Drakes	2 Dune Drakes fly overhead and attack with fire breath. Use the Dune Drake stat block.
12	Oasis	The party finds a small oasis with fresh water. Characters can fill their water skins and regain 1d4 hit points.
13	Old World Ruins	The party discovers a half-buried building. A successful DC 15 Investigation check reveals a hidden stash of supplies, including 1d4 rations and a purse of 25 gp.
14	Radioactive Zone	The party crosses a patch of irradiated ground. Each character must make a DC 13 Constitution saving throw or take 2d6 poison damage and gain one level of exhaustion.
15	Dehydration	The intense heat causes rapid dehydration. Each character must succeed on a DC 14 Constitution saving throw or gain one level of exhaustion.
16	Buried Treasure	PCs find a buried chest containing 100 gp worth of old world artifacts and a +1 weapon.
17	Swarmers	A swarm of mutated insects attacks. Use the Swarmers stat block.
18	Environmental Hazard	The ground collapses into a sinkhole. Each PC must make a DC 15 Dexterity saving throw or fall 20 feet, taking 2d6 bludgeoning damage.
19	Temporal Anomaly	The party stumbles into a pocket of warped time. Each character must make a DC 14 Wisdom saving throw. Those who fail experience rapid aging or de-aging (DM's choice), temporarily gaining or losing 1d20 years. This affects their physical appearance and grants advantage or disadvantage on Charisma checks for 1d4 hours until the effect wears off. A greater restoration spell can end this effect early.
20	Eerie Howls	The night is filled with eerie howls. Each character must succeed on a DC 12 Wisdom saving throw or suffer from the frightened condition until dawn.

Terrain and Environmental Hazards

The terrain of the Wasteland is harsh and unforgiving, characterized by cracked, dry earth, sparse vegetation, and scattered debris from the old world. The heat is oppressive, and the lack of shade makes travel exhausting.

Exhausting Heat: Each hour of travel requires a DC 7 Constitution saving throw. On a failed save, a character gains one level of exhaustion. Alternatively, use the Travel Pace rules of Forced March in the *Dungeon Master's Guide*, except start rolling after 4 hours a day instead of 8 (DC 10 + 1 for each hour past 4 hours).

Rough Terrain: Movement is halved in areas with dense debris or crumbling structures.

Cover: Debris and ruined structures can provide half cover (+2 to AC and Dexterity saving throws) or three-quarters cover (+5 to AC and Dexterity saving throws).

Lair Actions

On initiative count 20 (losing initiative ties), the Wasteland invokes one of the following lair actions:

Heat Wave: A sudden, intense heat wave sweeps across the area. Each creature must succeed on a DC 13 Constitution saving throw or take 2 (1d4) fire damage from severe sunburn and gain one level of exhaustion.

Dust Storm: A dust storm kicks up, obscuring vision. All creatures have disadvantage on attack rolls and Perception checks that rely on sight until the start of the next round.

Unearthed Relic: The shifting sands reveal a hidden cache of old-world artifacts. One PC of the DM's choice can find a useful item, such as a minor magical trinket or a piece of useful equipment.

Scaling the Encounter

Beginning Players (PC levels 1-5)

General Adjustments

- Reduce the number of enemies in encounters.
- Lower the damage and DCs for environmental hazards and lair actions.

Specific Adjustments

Encounters

- **Mutant Hound Pack**: Reduce to 1-2 Mutant Hounds.
- **Desperate Refugees**: Keep at 3 refugees.
- **Dust Storm**: DC 10 Constitution saving throw, damage 1d6.
- **Irradiated Pool**: DC 10 Constitution saving throw, damage 2d6.
- **Rad Beetles**: Reduce to 2 Rad Beetles.
- **Dune Drakes**: Remove fire breath or reduce damage to 1d6.
- **Swarmers**: Reduce the Swarmers' hit points to 40.

Terrain/Environmental Hazards

- **Exhausting Heat**: DC 6 Constitution saving throw.
- **Rough Terrain**: Movement is reduced by one-third instead of halved.

Lair Actions

- **Heat Wave**: DC 12 Constitution saving throw, damage 1d4 - 1.
- **Dust Storm**: Only disadvantage on Perception checks.
- **Unearthed Relic**: Minor magical trinket with very basic utility.

Intermediate Players (PC levels 6-10)

Use standard encounter setups as described.

Maintain original DCs and damage for environmental hazards and lair actions.

Advanced Players (PC levels 11+)

General Adjustments

- Increase the number of enemies in encounters.
- Raise the damage and DCs for environmental hazards and lair actions.

Specific Adjustments

Encounters:

- **Mutant Hound Pack**: Increase to 4-6 Mutant Hounds.
- **Desperate Refugees**: Increase to 10 refugees.
- **Dust Storm**: DC 16 Constitution saving throw, damage 3d6.
- **Irradiated Pool**: DC 15 Constitution saving throw, damage 4d6.
- **Rad Beetles**: Increase to 5-6 Rad Beetles.
- **Dune Drakes**: Increase fire breath damage to 3d6.
- **Swarmers**: Increase to 2 swarms.

Terrain/Environmental Hazards:

- **Exhausting Heat**: DC 8 Constitution saving throw.
- **Rough Terrain**: Increase movement penalty to include disadvantage on Dexterity saving throws.

Lair Actions:

- **Heat Wave**: DC 15 Constitution saving throw, damage 1d4+1.
- **Dust Storm**: Disadvantage on attack rolls, Perception checks, and Dexterity saving throws.
- **Unearthed Relic**: Valuable magical trinket or powerful piece of equipment.

Monsters

Mutant Hound (3)

Commoner, reduced hp (from the *PHB*) (3-5)

Survivor of Utopia

Rad Beetle (3)

Dune Drake (2)

Swarmers

Base Camp

The players receive their final briefing here from Engineer Liora about the Wall's crumbling section and the dangers that lie ahead. They must prepare for the journey while dealing with potential structural instability and old-world security drones.

You arrive at a bustling makeshift camp, a stark contrast to the desolate Wasteland you've traversed. The camp is alive with activity, as engineers and soldiers work tirelessly to maintain and monitor the Wall. The sound of clanging metal and the hum of generators fills the air. Tents and temporary structures are set up in a haphazard manner, creating a labyrinth of pathways. Sturdy barriers and makeshift fortifications stand guard around the perimeter, a testament to the camp's determination to withstand any threat.

At the center of the camp, you see a large tent with various tools and mechanical parts scattered around. Engineers huddle over blueprints and maps, deep in discussion. The Wall itself looms ominously in the background, its once imposing structure now marred by cracks and decay. The air here is thick with tension and urgency, as every person in the camp seems acutely aware of the looming danger. Your presence is met with nods of acknowledgement as you make your way towards the command tent, where you see a determined figure giving orders with a calm but authoritative voice.

Receive Mission Briefing

The PCs must interact with Engineer Liora to receive their final briefing and gather essential information about the Wall's crumbling section and the hazards they will face.

Interaction with Engineer Liora

Roleplaying Guidance:

- Engineer Liora is practical, focused, and a bit stern. She speaks with authority and precision, reflecting her deep knowledge and experience.

- Liora is deeply invested in the Wall's integrity and the mission's success. She will provide thorough details but expects the PCs to listen and understand the gravity of the situation.

Possible Dialogue Prompts:

- *"Welcome to the base camp. Time is of the essence, so let's get straight to it."*

- *"The Wall's crumbling section poses a significant threat. We've detected areas of severe structural weakness and old-world security drones that may still be operational."*

- *"Your mission is to cross the Wall and secure a path for our people. You must be prepared for both the instability of the Wall itself and the dangers lurking beyond."*

Sample Dialogue for Liora:

"Now, let's review the map. Here are the critical weak points in the Wall. You'll need to navigate these sections carefully to avoid triggering a collapse. Also, be aware of these marked areas – our scouts have reported old-world security drones that may still be operational. Approach them with caution."

"Once you're beyond the Wall, the terrain becomes even more unpredictable. Expect mutant creatures and environmental hazards. Use this map; it shows the safest routes we've identified so far. Any questions before you proceed?"

Key Information Provided by Liora

Structural Weaknesses:

- The Wall has multiple cracks and unstable sections. Avoid any heavy impacts that could trigger collapses.
- Specific areas to be wary of are marked on the map provided by Liora.

Old-World Security Drones:

- Some security drones may still be active. These drones can be dangerous but are also old and possibly malfunctioning.
- Use stealth or quick disabling tactics to avoid prolonged engagements with them.

Hazards Beyond the Wall:

- The area beyond the Wall is largely uncharted and dangerous. Expect mutant creatures and other environmental hazards.
- Liora provides a map with known landmarks and advises on potential safe routes.

Skill Challenges

Insight Check (DC 15):

- To gauge Liora's level of concern about specific threats.
- Success provides a deeper understanding of the most critical dangers.

Persuasion Check (DC 18):

- To request additional supplies or specific equipment.
- Success grants an extra piece of useful gear (e.g., climbing equipment, extra rations, or a minor magical item).

Investigation Check (DC 14):

- To review the maps and blueprints for hidden details.
- Success reveals an alternative, potentially safer path or an area with useful salvage.

History Check (DC 16):

- To recall knowledge about old-world security systems and drones.
- Success provides advantage on any future checks related to disabling or avoiding Security Drones.

Terrain

The terrain within the camp is a mix of makeshift pathways, cluttered work areas, and temporary fortifications.

Cluttered Pathways: Moving through the camp at normal speed requires a DC 10 Dexterity (Athletics or Acrobatics) check to deftly step around tools and debris. Failure results in movement being halved for that turn.

Fortifications: Barriers and fortifications provide half cover (+2 to AC and Dexterity saving throws) or three-quarters cover (+5 to AC and Dexterity saving throws) depending on their size.

Structural Instability: Areas near the Wall are unstable. Any heavy impact (such as a critical hit or explosive spell) may cause debris to fall. Each creature within 10 feet of the Wall must make a DC 14 Dexterity saving throw or take 2d6 bludgeoning damage.

Lair Actions

On initiative count 20 (losing initiative ties), the Base Camp invokes one of the following lair actions:

Security Drone Activation: Old-world security drones activate. Roll a d6; on a 4-6, 1d4 Security Drones join the encounter.

Wall Tremors: The Wall shakes violently. Each creature must succeed on a DC 13 Dexterity saving throw or be knocked prone.

Repair Surge: Engineer Liora can direct a surge of repair energy. One construct or mechanical device within 30 feet regains 20 hit points.

Scaling the Encounter

Beginning Players (PC levels 1-5)

- Reduce the number and strength of enemies.
- Lower the DCs for skill checks and environmental hazards.
- Simplify lair actions and reduce damage output.

Intermediate Players (PC levels 6-10)

- Use standard encounter setups as described.
- Maintain original DCs and damage for skill checks and environmental hazards.
- Use standard lair actions and damage output.

Advanced Players (PC levels 11+)

- Increase the number and strength of enemies.
- Raise the DCs for skill checks and environmental hazards.
- Enhance lair actions and increase damage output.

Monster

Security Drone (1d4)

NPC

Engineer Liora: The chief engineer overseeing the Wall's maintenance, who provides technical insight and warns about potential hazards. Her expertise and leadership are crucial to the camp's operations and the PCs' mission.

Act 2

Act 2 – On the Wall

Climbing the Wall

The PCs start at the base of the Wall, a mile-high structure that stretches from horizon to horizon. They must climb the Wall, encountering various challenges such as crumbling sections and an old security gate to reach the top and continue their quest.

You stand at the base of an immense wall, its sheer height disappearing into the clouds above and stretching endlessly in both directions. The Wall is a monolithic structure, constructed from a mix of ancient stone and decaying metal. A thousand feet above you, you can see sections where the Wall appears to be crumbling, with large chunks missing and debris scattered near the base all around you.

The ground around you is dry and cracked, a testament to the harsh conditions of the Wasteland. The air is thick with dust, and the heat from the sun beats down relentlessly. As you prepare to begin your ascent, you notice the remains of old climbing gear and makeshift ladders left behind by previous climbers. The task ahead is daunting, but it is the only way to uncover the secrets that lie beyond the Wall and secure a future for your people.

Climb the Wall

The party must navigate the treacherous climb up the Wall, dealing with environmental hazards, crumbling sections, and old-world security measures. This activity is crucial for progressing to the next part of their journey in the *Beyond the Wall* adventure.

Climbing Mechanics

Climbing Check: Climbing the Wall requires a DC 15 Strength (Athletics) check. PCs without climbing gear make this check with disadvantage.

Falling: On a failed check, the character falls 20 feet before catching themselves, taking 2d6 bludgeoning damage. They must succeed on another DC 15 Strength (Athletics) check to stop the fall and regain their position.

Assistance: PCs can assist each other. A character providing assistance must succeed on a DC 10 Strength (Athletics) check to be able to perform the Help action for another climber. Success grants the other character advantage on their next climbing check.

Distance and Time

Measuring Distance:

- The Wall is one mile high (5,280 feet).

- PCs can climb at half their movement speed per round (e.g., a character with 30 ft. speed climbs 15 feet per round).

- One round (6 seconds) = 15 feet (for a character with a 30 ft. speed).

- One minute (10 rounds) = 150 feet.

- One hour (600 rounds) = 9,000 feet (150 feet per minute x 60 minutes).

Climbing Time:

With an average speed of 30 feet, in a perfect world (flawless Strength, endless Constitution, and no other factors causing slowdown (such as falling debris or combat encounters), it would take about 35.2 minutes of climbing to reach the top.

More practically, the vast majority of PCs cannot sustain sheer vertical climbing at maximum speed for very long. Unless characters (or their magic items) are specifically suited to vertical climbing or flying, they need to rest and conserve their energy during such a long, arduous activity. Additionally, the party may face encounters such as bad weather or deteriorating Wall sections. Considering these factors, a more realistic climbing time for an average party using climbing gear is 5-6 hours.

1d6 Random Encounter Table

1d6	Name of the Encounter	Description
1	Falling Debris	**Description:** Sections of the Wall are unstable and prone to collapse. **Trigger:** Passing through a crumbling section. **Activation:** Automatic when passing through. **Effect:** Each creature in the affected section must make a DC 14 Dexterity saving throw. On a failure, the creature takes 2d6 bludgeoning damage and falls 20 feet. **Detection:** DC 15 Wisdom (Perception) check to notice the section's instability. **Disable:** Cannot be disabled, must be avoided or navigated carefully.
2	Security Drone Attack	**Description:** Old-world Security Drones activate and attack the climbers. **Effect:** Roll a d6; on a 4-6, 1d4 Security Drones appear and attack the PCs. **Combat Encounter:** PCs must fight or disable the drones with a DC 15 Dexterity (Technology) check using thieves' tools OR Intelligence (Technology) check using engineer's tools.
3	Gusting Winds	**Description:** A sudden strong gust of wind threatens to knock the climbers off balance. **Effect:** Each character must make a DC 14 Strength saving throw to maintain their grip. On a failure, they are pushed 5 feet to the side and must make a DC 15 Strength (Athletics) check to avoid falling 20 feet and taking 2d6 bludgeoning damage.
4	Hidden Nest	**Description:** The PCs disturb a nest of mutated birds while climbing. **Effect:** 1d4 giant eagles (as found in the *PHB*, but with added mutation traits such as dealing an additional 1d6 poison damage) attack the party, defending their nest. **Combat Encounter:** PCs must either fight off the birds or try to calm them with a DC 15 Wisdom (Animal Handling) check.
5	Exposed Pipeline	**Description:** An old pipeline with a hidden electrified surface. **Trigger:** Touching the pipeline. **Activation:** Automatic upon touch. **Effect:** Each creature touching the pipeline takes 3d6 lightning damage. **Detection:** DC 15 Intelligence (Investigation) check to notice the electrical hazard. **Disable:** DC 15 Dexterity (Technology) check using thieves' tools or Intelligence (Technology) check using engineer's tools.
6	Ancient Glyphs	**Description:** PCs find ancient glyphs that provide a magical benefit if deciphered. **Effect:** A DC 15 Intelligence (Arcana) check reveals the glyphs' benefits, granting advantage on skill checks made to climb for the next hour or providing a one-time 2d8 healing to each PC who studies them. **Discovery Encounter:** PCs benefit from the magical boost if successful.

Climbing the Wall

As the party ascends the Wall, they will encounter various challenges at specific heights. The Wall is one mile high (5,280 feet), and each major encounter occurs at predetermined intervals. Below are the instructions for when the PCs will reach each encounter:

The Lifeline Pipeline (500 feet up)

Location: The party finds the Lifeline Pipeline at approximately 500 feet (about 10% of the total height).

Description: A network of ancient, rusted pipelines running through the Wall, once used to transport water and other resources. The pipelines are now mostly dry and corroded, but some sections still hold traces of their original purpose.

Challenge: Players must navigate through the maze-like network to find clues about the water source and possibly restore some functionality to aid their mission. This involves a series of DC 15 Intelligence (Investigation) checks. Failing a check may result in getting lost, requiring additional time to find the way out.

Additional Details: Pipemaster Jax, an old-world engineer, resides here and can provide guidance and knowledge about the pipeline's layout and potential shortcuts.

The Crumbling Section (1,000 feet up)

Location: The party encounters the Crumbling Section at approximately 1,000 feet (about 20% of the total height).

Description: A dangerously unstable part of the Wall with large cracks and missing chunks, posing a significant risk to those attempting to cross. Additionally, the dragon-like Dune Drakes nesting near the section will viciously defend their territory from the encroaching party.

Challenge: The PCs must navigate this section to get beyond the Wall, facing the immediate danger of falling debris and structural collapse. This requires a series of DC 15 Dexterity (Athletics or Acrobatics) checks to carefully climb without dislodging debris. Each failure results in falling debris and a DC 13 Dexterity saving throw to avoid 2d6 bludgeoning damage.

Additional Details: PCs might find clues or messages left by previous explorers.

The Old Security Gate (2,000 feet up)

Location: The PCs reach the Old Security Gate at approximately 2,000 feet (about 40% of the total height).

Description: An ancient, rusted gate embedded in the Wall, with remnants of old-world security systems that can still pose a threat to intruders.

Challenge: Players must decide whether to disable the security systems or find another way. Disabling the gate's security system requires defeating or bypassing old-world security drones, a laser grid, and solving several logic puzzles.. Failure triggers an alarm, summoning 1d4 Security Drones.

Additional Details: The gate provides an alternative, albeit risky, way to cross the Wall.

The Hidden Armory (3,000 feet up)

Location: The party discovers the Hidden Armory at approximately 3,000 feet (about 60% of the total height).

Description: A concealed chamber within the Wall, accessible through a hidden entrance obscured by rubble and overgrowth. The Armory contains weapons and equipment from the prc-apocalypse era.

Challenge: Accessing the Armory requires solving a series of DC 15 Intelligence (Investigation) or Wisdom (Perception) checks to find and open the entrance. Inside, PCs may find valuable old-world weapons and gear. The Armory is not unguarded and poses significant challenges.

Additional Details: PCs might find a recorded message or hologram from a former soldier, providing instructions on how to unlock the Armory and use its contents.

The Guardian's Perch (Top of the Wall, 5,280 feet)

Location: The PCs reach the Guardian's Perch at the very top of the Wall (5,280 feet).

Description: A high vantage point atop the Wall, where ancient guardians once stood watch. The perch provides a panoramic view of the surrounding Wasteland and the Wall itself, offering strategic insight into potential threats and pathways.

Challenge: Reaching the perch requires a final series of DC 15 Strength (Athletics) checks. The perch attracts flying mutated creatures, requiring the players to defend themselves while climbing. Navigational puzzles to safely reach the top, involving climbing and balance checks, as well as deciphering old maps and codes left by the ancient guardians.

Additional Details: Skywatcher Finn, a reclusive scout, has made the perch his home. Finn possesses valuable information about the terrain and dangers beyond the Wall and can be persuaded to assist the players.

Climbing Sequence

- **0-500 feet:** Regular climbing checks with potential random encounters.

- **500 feet:** Find the Lifeline Pipeline.

- **500-1,000 feet:** Continue climbing checks with potential random encounters.
- **1,000 feet:** Encounter the Crumbling Section.
- **1,000-2,000 feet:** Continue climbing with potential random encounters.
- **2,000 feet:** Encounter the Old Security Gate.
- **2,000-3,000 feet:** Continue climbing with potential random encounters.
- **3,000 feet:** Discover the Hidden Armory.
- **3,000-5,280 feet:** Final stretch of climbing with potential random encounters.
- **5,280 feet:** Reach the Guardian's Perch.

Preparing for the Descent

When the PCs have reached the top of the Wall, the descent down the far side of the Wall should be faster but still present challenges. The Wall is 100 feet wide at the top, providing ample space for the party to prepare their descent.

Preparation

Rope and Climbing Gear: PCs can use rope and climbing gear to make their descent easier. Each character should secure themselves with a rope, anchoring it to stable structures or spikes on top of the Wall.

Check for Hazards: PCs should spend time examining the Wall's surface on the descent side. An occasional DC 15 Wisdom (Perception) or Intelligence (Investigation) check will reveal potential hazards and the best routes to take.

Mechanics for Descending the Wall

Controlled Descent: PCs can rappel down using ropes, moving at their climbing speed (half their normal speed). This requires a DC 10 Strength (Athletics) check. Failure results in slipping but catching themselves without taking damage.

Fast Descent: PCs can choose to descend faster, moving at their full speed but with an increased difficulty. This requires a DC 15 Strength (Athletics)

check. Failure results in falling 20 feet and taking 2d6 bludgeoning damage.

Falling: If a PC falls, they must make a DC 15 Strength (Athletics) check to stop their fall after 20 feet. If they fail, they fall an additional 20 feet, taking 2d6 bludgeoning damage for every 20 feet fallen.

Time Calculation:

Controlled Descent (for a character with a 30 ft. speed, who moves 15 feet per round):

- One round (6 seconds) = 15 feet
- One minute (10 rounds) = 150 feet
- One hour (600 rounds) = 9,000 feet (150 feet per minute * 60 minutes)
- Descending the Wall (5,280 feet) takes approximately 35.2 minutes of climbing time.

Speed Descent:

- One round (6 seconds) = 30 feet
- One minute (10 rounds) = 300 feet
- One hour (600 rounds) = 18,000 feet (300 feet per minute * 60 minutes)
- Descending the Wall (5,280 feet) takes approximately 17.6 minutes of climbing time.

With an average speed of 30 feet, in a perfect world (flawless Strength, endless Constitution, and no other factors causing slowdown such as falling debris or combat encounters, it would take about 35.2 minutes of controlled descent, or 17.6 minutes of speed descent, to reach the base of the Wall.

More practically, most PCs cannot sustain sheer vertical descent at full speed for very long, even when rappelling down. Unless characters (or their magic items) are specifically suited to vertical climbing or flying, they need to rest and conserve their energy during such a long activity. Additionally, the party may face encounters such as bad weather or deteriorating Wall sections, rendering it unsafe to descend even at a controlled speed. Considering these factors, a more realistic descent time for an average party using climbing gear to rappel is 2-3 hours.

Found Items to Speed Up Descent

Name	Description	Instructions	Assembly or Attunement	Location
Paraglider	A foldable fabric wing with a frame, resembling a large kite. Helps glide down the Wall safely.	Usage: Requires a DC 12 Dexterity (Acrobatics) check to control the descent. Move 60 feet per round.	Assembly: DC 14 Intelligence (Investigation) check to put together if found in pieces.	Hidden in a supply crate at the top of the Wall. DC 15 Wisdom (Perception) check to find.
Boots of Feather Falling	Magical boots that reduce fall speed. Appear as sturdy leather boots with light feather motifs.	Usage: Wearing these boots slows descent, preventing fall damage and allowing safe landing. Move 30 feet per round.	Attunement: Requires attunement. Wondrous item, rare.	Found near a hidden cache marked by ancient glyphs. DC 15 Intelligence (Arcana) check to reveal.
Spider Climb Gloves	Magical gloves that allow the wearer to stick to and climb surfaces effortlessly. Made of dark, supple leather with web-like stitching.	Usage: Wearing these gloves grants the Spider Climb ability, allowing movement on vertical surfaces without checks. Move 30 feet per round.	Attunement: Requires attunement. Wondrous item, uncommon.	Hidden in a small alcove at the top of the Wall. DC 15 Wisdom (Perception) check to locate.
Rope of Entanglement (Cursed)	A seemingly normal rope that can entangle enemies but curses the user. Appears as a 50-foot length of sturdy rope.	Usage: Can be used to rappel down safely, moving 15 feet per round. Curse: Once used, the user must make a DC 15 Wisdom saving throw or be unable to let go of the rope, becoming entangled themselves and needing assistance to get free.	Attunement: Requires attunement and triggers the curse upon use. Wondrous item, rare.	Coiled around an old gear mechanism. DC 13 Wisdom (Perception) check to find.
Wind Rider Amulet	A magical amulet shaped like a winged creature. Grants the ability to glide safely down.	Usage: , When the wearer falls, they instead glide down at 60 feet per round, and take no damage from falling.	Attunement: Requires attunement. Wondrous item, rare.	Hidden under a loose stone at the top of the Wall. DC 15 Intelligence (Investigation) check to discover.

Lair Actions

On initiative count 20 (losing initiative ties), the Wall invokes one of the following lair actions:

Falling Debris: Debris falls from a crumbling section of the Wall. Each creature directly on or below the crumbling Wall section who is within 10 feet horizontally of the fall area must make a DC 14 Dexterity saving throw or take 2d6 bludgeoning damage and fall 20 feet.

Security Drone Activation: Dormant security drones activate. Roll a d6; on a 4-6, 1d4 Security Drones join the encounter.

Unstable Footing: The Wall shifts slightly. Each creature climbing must make a DC 13 Strength (Athletics) check or lose their grip and fall 20 feet, taking 2d6 bludgeoning damage.

Scaling the Encounter

Beginning Players (PC levels 1-5)

General Adjustments

- Reduce the number and strength of encounters.

- Lower the DCs for skill checks.

- Simplify lair actions and reduce damage output.

Specific Adjustments

Climbing Mechanics

- **Climbing Check**: DC 10 Strength (Athletics) check to ascend.

- **Falling**. On a failed check, fall 10 feet, taking 1d6 bludgeoning damage. DC 10 Strength (Athletics) check to stop the fall.

Distance and Time

- Reduce number of Strength (Athletics) checks required for the climb.

Random Encounters

- **Falling Debris**: DC 12 Dexterity saving throw, 1d6 bludgeoning damage.

- **Security Drone Attack**: 1-2 Security Drones.

- **Gusting Winds**: DC 12 Strength saving throw, pushed 5 feet, DC 12 Strength (Athletics) check.

- **Hidden Nest**: 1-2 giant eagles (no additional poison damage).
- **Exposed Pipeline**: 2d6 lightning damage.

Ancient Glyphs: DC 12 Intelligence (Arcana) check, advantage on skill checks made to climb for 30 minutes or 1d8 healing.

Major Encounters

- **Lifeline Pipeline** (500 feet): DC 10 Intelligence (Investigation) checks.
- **Crumbling Section** (1,000 feet): DC 10 Dexterity checks, DC 10 Dexterity saving throw, 1d6 bludgeoning damage.
- **Old Security Gate** (2,000 feet): DC 10 Intelligence (Investigation) checks or Dexterity checks using thieves' tools, 1 Security Drone.
- **Hidden Armory** (3,000 feet): DC 10 Intelligence (Investigation) or Wisdom (Perception) check.

Guardian's Perch (5,280 feet): DC 10 Strength (Athletics) checks, fewer flying mutated creatures.

Lair Actions

- **Falling Debris**: DC 12 Dexterity saving throw, 1d6 bludgeoning damage.
- **Security Drone Activation**: 1 Security Drone.
- **Unstable Footing**: DC 12 Strength (Athletics) check, fall 10 feet, 1d6 bludgeoning damage.

Intermediate Players (PC levels 6-10)

- Use standard encounter setups as described.
- Maintain original DCs and damage for skill checks and environmental hazards.

Advanced Players (PC levels 11+)

General Adjustments

- Increase the number and strength of encounters.
- Raise the DCs for skill checks.
- Enhance lair actions and increase damage output.

Specific Adjustments

Climbing Mechanics

- **Climbing Check**: DC 20 Strength (Athletics) check to ascend.

- **Falling**: On a failed check, fall 30 feet, taking 3d6 bludgeoning damage. DC 20 Strength (Athletics) check to stop the fall.

Random Encounters

- **Falling Debris**: DC 16 Dexterity saving throw, 3d6 bludgeoning damage.
- **Security Drone Attack**: 2d4 Security Drones.
- **Gusting Winds**: DC 16 Strength saving throw, pushed 10 feet, DC 20 Strength (Athletics) check.
- **Hidden Nest**: 1d4+2 giant eagles (with enhanced poison damage).
- **Exposed Pipeline**: 4d6 lightning damage.
- **Ancient Glyphs**: DC 18 Intelligence (Arcana) check, advantage on skill checks made to climb for 1 hour or 2d10 healing.

Major Encounters

- **Lifeline Pipeline** (500 feet): DC 20 Intelligence (Investigation) checks.
- **Crumbling Section** (1,000 feet): DC 20 Dexterity checks, DC 16 Dexterity saving throw, 3d6 bludgeoning damage.
- **Old Security Gate** (2,000 feet): DC 20 Intelligence (Investigation) or Dexterity check using thieves' tools, 2d4 Security Drones.
- **Hidden Armory** (3,000 feet): DC 20 Intelligence (Investigation) or Wisdom (Perception) check.
- **Guardian's Perch** (5,280 feet): DC 20 Strength (Athletics) checks, increased number of flying mutated creatures.

Lair Actions

- **Falling Debris**: DC 16 Dexterity saving throw, 3d6 bludgeoning damage.
- **Security Drone Activation**: 2d4 Security Drones.
- **Unstable Footing**: DC 16 Strength (Athletics) check, fall 30 feet, 3d6 bludgeoning damage.

Monsters

Security Drone (1d4)

Giant Eagle, mutated (from the *PHB*) (1d4)

The Lifeline Pipeline

The players must navigate the maze-like network of ancient pipelines, dealing with Toxic Sludge monsters and solving puzzles to restore functionality. They will encounter Pipemaster Jax, who can offer crucial guidance and knowledge about the pipeline's layout and shortcuts and explain the components necessary to repair this major structure.

You see above you a series of massive pipes emerging from the Wall, each one about eight feet in diameter and large enough to walk through. The pipes stretch into the darkness, with echoes of dripping water and the distant hum of old machinery filling the air. Rust and corrosion cover the surfaces, and the smell of damp metal and decay is overwhelming. Moss and vines cling to the outsides of the pipes, adding an eerie, natural touch to the ancient infrastructure.

As you peer into the darkness of the pipes, you see that some lead to complete dead ends while others seem to stretch on endlessly. Symbols and markings are etched into the metal near the openings, possibly clues left by previous explorers. You can sense a lingering presence, as if the pipelines themselves are watching, waiting to test your resolve and ingenuity.

Activities

Navigate the Maze: Players must solve a physical maze puzzle, representing the complex network of pipelines.

Encounter Toxic Sludges: At key intervals, PCs will be attacked by Toxic Sludges.

Consult with Pipemaster Jax: The party will encounter Pipemaster Jax, who can offer insights and shortcuts, and describe the tasks and components necessary to repair the Lifeline Pipeline.

Navigate the Maze

Physical Representation

- Provide players with a map or visual representation of the maze. There are two versions available: one basic and one advanced.

- The basic maze is less complex and shorter, ideal for newer or less experienced players.

- The advanced maze is more intricate, with multiple layers, false paths, and additional challenges for experienced players.

Time Pressure

- Set a time limit for players to solve the maze to add urgency and tension. Depending on the group's experience, a reasonable time limit could be 10-15 minutes.

- Use the following table to determine when encounters happen based on how long the players take to solve the puzzle:

Time Elapsed (Minutes)	Encounter Triggered
5	Corrosive Eruption (Lair Action)
10	Toxic Sludge Attack
15	Structural Instability (Lair Action)

Starting Point

- PCs enter the maze from the base of the pipeline network. Describe the entrance as a dark, damp tunnel with corroded walls and the distant sound of dripping water echoing through the passages.

Choosing Paths

- Players must choose which path to take at each junction.

- Encourage them to use their skills (e.g., Intelligence checks for remembering details or Wisdom (Perception) checks for noticing subtle signs or symbols left by previous explorers).

Encounters

- As players navigate the maze, they will encounter Toxic Sludges at key intervals.

- Describe the encounters vividly and engage PCs in combat or creative problem-solving to bypass the threats.

Solving the Maze

- Players need to make decisions at each junction within the maze.

- At critical decision points, require PCs to make an Intelligence (Investigation) or Wisdom (Perception) check (DC 14) to find clues or signs that guide them toward the correct path.

- Provide hints or partial clues for successful checks. For example, PCs might notice a faint arrow etched into the pipeline wall or find a note left by a previous explorer.

Finding Pipemaster Jax

- Jax is located at a central point in the maze, near a large junction where multiple pipes converge.

- To find Jax, PCs must make a successful Intelligence (Investigation) check (DC 15) to notice signs of recent activity and follow the clues to his location.

- When they find Jax, he can provide valuable information about the maze, shortcuts, and how to handle the Toxic Sludges.

Consult with Pipemaster Jax

PCs will encounter Pipemaster Jax, who can offer insights and shortcuts and explain what's needed to restore the Lifeline Pipeline to working order.

Encounter Location: Pipemaster Jax is located at a central point in the maze, near a large junction where multiple pipes converge. To find Jax, players must make a successful Intelligence (Investigation) check (DC 15) to notice signs of recent activity and follow the clues to his location.

Description of Pipemaster Jax's Area:

- The area is cluttered with makeshift tools and parts, indicating someone's been living and working here for a long time.

- There are notes and schematics pinned to the walls, and a small, flickering light illuminates the workspace.

Information Shared by Jax

Solve the Maze

Jax explains that the PCs must solve the maze to find the path that goes through the Wall. He provides hints about the maze's layout and warns them of the dangers they might face.

"This pipeline system was designed as a maze to deter thieves and marauders. To get through, you need to find the correct path. I'll give you a tip: follow the flow of air and listen for the faint sound of water."

Water Flow Requirements

Jax outlines the necessary steps to ensure water flows through the pipes. He mentions that they will need to find a pump, power source, and access to clean water.

"Long ago, these pipes once provided fresh water to the territories facing the Wall, but that source is now long dried up. To restore the water flow through these pipes, you'll need three things: a pump, a power source, and clean water. You might be able to find usable parts in ruins of an old-world urban region, like a city. Finding usable power and clean water will be the tricky part. We don't know what's out there."

Jax's Assistance

Jax offers to join the party on their journey, providing them with advantage on repairing the pump, connecting the power, and ensuring the water flows properly.

"I can help you navigate this maze and get everything working. If you need to repair the pump or connect the power, I can give you a hand. You'll find that having someone with my expertise is invaluable in a place like this."

Advantages Provided by Jax

Advantage on Repairs: While Jax is with the PCs, they have advantage on any Intelligence (Arcana) or Dexterity (Technology) checks to repair the pump.

Advantage on Power Connections: Jax's presence grants advantage on Intelligence (Arcana) or Wisdom (Survival) checks to connect and secure the power source.

Ensuring Water Flow: Jax provides advantage on any checks related to ensuring the water flows through the pipeline once everything is set up.

Terrain

The terrain within the pipeline network is damp, slippery, and unstable. Many sections are corroded and can collapse underfoot.

Slippery Ground: Moving at normal speed requires a DC 12 Dexterity (Acrobatics) check to avoid slipping. Running or moving quickly requires a DC 15 Dexterity (Athletics or Acrobatics) check.

Unstable Terrain: Corroded or collapsed sections require a DC 14 Strength (Athletics) check to navigate or clear.

Lair Actions

On initiative count 20 (losing initiative ties), the Lifeline Pipeline invokes one of the following lair actions:

Corrosive Eruption: A burst of Toxic Sludge erupts from a nearby pipe. Each creature within 10 feet must make a DC 14 Dexterity saving throw or take 10 (3d6) acid damage and be knocked prone.

Structural Instability: The pipeline shakes violently, causing debris to fall. Each creature must make a DC 13 Dexterity saving throw or take 7 (2d6) bludgeoning damage.

Toxic Vapors: A cloud of toxic vapors fills a 20-foot radius area. Each creature must make a DC 14 Constitution saving throw or be poisoned for 1 minute. While poisoned, the creature takes 5 (1d10) poison damage at the start of each of its turns.

Scaling the Encounter

Beginning Players (PC levels 1-5)

General Adjustments

- Simplify the maze and reduce the number of Toxic Sludge encounters.
- Lower the DCs for skill checks and saves.
- Decrease the damage output of traps and monsters.

Specific Adjustments

Navigate the Maze

- Simplify the maze with fewer junctions.
- DC 12 for Intelligence (Investigation) or Wisdom (Perception) checks to find the correct path.

Encounters

- **Toxic Sludges**: Reduce the number of sludges to 1-2 with lower stats.
- **Attack**: +3 to hit, 1d6 acid damage.
- DC 12 Constitution save for poison effects.

- Reduce the number of encounters to once every 10 minutes.

Consult with Pipemaster Jax

- Jax provides more direct guidance with simpler instructions.
- Advantage on DC 12 checks for repairs and connections.

Lair Actions

- **Corrosive Eruption**: DC 12 Dexterity save or take 2d6 acid damage.
- **Structural Instability**: DC 11 Dexterity save or take 1d6 bludgeoning damage.
- **Toxic Vapors**: DC 12 Constitution save or be poisoned for 1 minute, 1d6 poison damage per turn.

Intermediate Players (PC levels 6-10)

- Use standard maze complexity and encounter frequency.
- Maintain original DCs and damage for skill checks and environmental hazards.

Advanced Players (PC levels 11+)

General Adjustments

- Increase the complexity of the maze and the number of Toxic Sludge encounters.
- Raise the DCs for skill checks and saves.
- Enhance the damage output of traps and monsters.

Specific Adjustments

Navigate the Maze

- Complex maze with multiple layers and false paths.

- DC 16 for Intelligence (Investigation) or Wisdom (Perception) checks to find the correct path.

Encounters

- **Toxic Sludges**: Increase number to 3-4 with enhanced stats.

- **Attack**: +6 to hit, 2d6 acid damage.

- DC 16 Constitution save for poison effects.

- Increase encounter frequency (every 5 minutes).

Consult with Pipemaster Jax

- Jax provides cryptic clues requiring interpretation.

- Advantage on DC 16 checks for repairs and connections.

Lair Actions

- **Corrosive Eruption**: DC 16 Dexterity save or take 4d6 acid damage.

- **Structural Instability**: DC 15 Dexterity save or take 3d6 bludgeoning damage.

- **Toxic Vapors**: DC 16 Constitution save or be poisoned for 1 minute, 2d6 poison damage per turn.

Monster

Toxic Sludge (2-3)

NPC

Pipemaster Jax: This pipeline engineer offers crucial guidance and knowledge about the pipeline's layout and shortcuts and explains what's needed to restore the Lifeline Pipeline to working order.

The Crumbling Section

The players must navigate through a dangerously unstable part of the Wall, dealing with falling debris and potential structural collapse. This section is also a nesting area for territorial Dune Drakes, adding further danger.

As you continue your ascent, the Wall before you begins to show signs of severe deterioration. Large cracks spiderweb across its surface, and entire sections seem to be missing, revealing the inner structure of the Wall. The air is filled with the sounds of shifting stone and falling debris, making every step up a cautious one. The sun casts long shadows, and you can see that this part of the Wall is treacherously unstable.

Suddenly, you notice movement from the cracks and crevices. Small, dragon-like creatures with scales that shimmer like desert sand emerge from their hiding spots. Their piercing yellow eyes lock onto you, and a low growl emanates from their throats. The air grows hotter, and you can sense the impending danger from their fiery breath.

Activities

Navigate the Crumbling Section: PCs must make a series of DC 15 Dexterity (Athletics or Acrobatics) checks to avoid falling debris and maintain their footing on the unstable Wall.

Clues Left by Previous Explorers: PCs might find messages or clues etched into the Wall or written on scraps of parchment, giving hints about the dangers ahead and possible safe routes.

Encounter with the Dune Drakes: As the party navigates the unstable terrain, they will inevitably attract the attention of the Dune Drakes.

Navigate the Crumbling Section

The players must carefully navigate the unstable terrain of the Crumbling Section of the Wall. This involves a series of skill checks and strategic decisions to avoid falling debris, crumbling ground, and other hazards. This activity challenges the PCs' dexterity, teamwork, and quick thinking as they traverse this treacherous section.

Skill Checks and Hazards

Initial Ascent

- **Check**: Each character must make a DC 15 Dexterity (Athletics or Acrobatics) check.
- **Success**: The character moves safely across the unstable ground.
- **Failure**: The character loses their footing, falls 20 feet and takes 2d6 bludgeoning damage.

Falling Debris

- **Frequency**: At the start of each PC's turn, they must make a DC 12 Dexterity saving throw.
- **Success**: The character avoids the falling debris.
- **Failure**: The character takes 2d6 bludgeoning damage from falling rocks and falls 20 feet.

Cracked Pathways

- **Check**: As PCs move through the section, they encounter cracked pathways. Each PC must make a DC 14 Dexterity (Athletics or Acrobatics) check to cross these safely.
- **Success**: Thecharacter crosses the cracked pathway without incident.
- **Failure**: The character falls into a crevice, taking 1d6 bludgeoning damage and becoming restrained. They must make a DC 12 Strength (Athletics) check to climb out.

Balancing Acts

- **Check**: Occasionally, PCs must balance on narrow ledges. Each PC must make a DC 15 Dexterity (Acrobatics) check to maintain their balance.
- **Success**: The character maintains their balance and continues moving.
- **Failure**: The character slips and falls, taking 2d6 bludgeoning damage. They must immediately make a DC 12 Dexterity saving throw to catch themselves on the narrow ledge and avoid falling further.

Strategic Decisions

PCs can choose to:

Move Cautiously: Moving at half speed grants advantage on all Dexterity (Acrobatics) checks but takes longer to climb.

Rush Through: Moving at full speed risks disadvantage on all checks but reduces the time spent in danger.

Teamwork Opportunities

Assisting Each Other: PCs can use the Help action to grant advantage to another PC's check.

Using Ropes: PCs can use ropes to secure themselves, reducing the risk of falling. Using a rope grants a +2 bonus to Dexterity (Athletics or Acrobatics) checks.

Clue Left by Previous Explorers

As PCs explore the Crumbling Section, they may discover clues left by previous explorers that can provide valuable insights or warnings. These clues can be found etched into the Wall, written on scraps of parchment, or hidden in notebooks. To find and decipher these clues, PCs must succeed on appropriate skill checks. Each clue offers benefits to PCs who successfully interpret them.

Discovery of Clues

Etched Message: "Beware the drakes. They guard their nests fiercely."

- **DC to Find:** 15 Intelligence (Investigation) check
- **DC to Decipher:** 12 Intelligence (History) or Wisdom (Survival) check
- **Effect:** Provides PCs with forewarning about the Dune Drakes. Grants advantage on the first initiative roll against the drakes.
- **Location:** Etched into a large stone near the base of the Wall.

Scrap of Parchment: "Found a safe path to the east. Stay low and move quickly."

- **DC to Find:** 12 Wisdom (Perception) check
- **DC to Decipher:** 10 Intelligence (Investigation) or Wisdom (Survival) check
- **Effect:** Provides guidance on navigating the unstable terrain. PCs following this advice gain a +2 bonus on Dexterity (Athletics or Acrobatics) checks to avoid falling debris.
- **Location:** Tucked under a loose stone at the edge of a ledge.

Carved Symbol: An arrow pointing toward a safer route, with a note: "Follow this path to avoid the worst of the crumbling sections."

- **DC to Find:** 14 Wisdom (Perception) check
- **DC to Decipher:** 12 Intelligence (Investigation) or Wisdom (Survival) check
- **Effect:** Helps characters find the safest path through the Crumbling Section. PCs who follow the path have advantage on all Dexterity (Athletics or Acrobatics) checks to navigate the terrain.
- **Location:** Carved into the Wall itself at a junction where the path splits.

Hidden Notebook Entry: "The Old Security Gate is still active. Disable the drones before proceeding."

- **DC to Find:** 16 Intelligence (Investigation) check
- **DC to Decipher:** 12 Intelligence (Arcana) or Intelligence (Technology) check
- **Effect:** Alerts PCs to the dangers of the Old Security Gate. Grants advantage on the first check to disable security systems.
- **Location:** Hidden in a crevice behind a loose rock.

Graffiti on the Wall's Rocky Face: "Pipeline below essential for water transport. Be prepared to repair."

- **DC to Find:** 13 Wisdom (Perception) check
- **DC to Decipher:** 12 Intelligence (Investigation) or Wisdom (Survival) check
- **Effect:** Informs PCs about the Lifeline Pipeline. Grants advantage on first check to repair the pipeline.
- **Location:** Scrawled on a section of the Wall just above a large crack.

Parchment Note: "Dune Drakes avoid smoke. Create a diversion to pass safely."

- **DC to Find:** 11 Wisdom (Perception) check
- **DC to Decipher:** 10 Intelligence (Arcana) or Wisdom (Nature) check
- **Effect:** Provides the party with a strategy to avoid Dune Drakes. Grants advantage on Stealth checks to avoid the drakes.
- **Location:** Caught in a crevice near a small ledge, partially hidden by debris.

Etched Map: "Safe spots marked. Use them to rest and regroup."

- **DC to Find:** 15 Intelligence (Investigation) check
- **DC to Decipher:** 12 Intelligence (History) or Wisdom (Survival) check
- **Effect:** Shows locations of safe spots in the Crumbling Section. Grants advantage on checks to find safe resting places while ascending the Wall.
- **Location:** Etched into a flat section of the Wall near a natural resting spot.

Old Journal Page: "The Wall's cracks lead to hidden passages. Search thoroughly."

- **DC to Find:** 14 Intelligence (Investigation) check
- **DC to Decipher:** 12 Intelligence (History) or Wisdom (Survival) check
- **Effect:** Reveals hidden passages within the Wall. Grants advantage on checks to locate hidden passages while ascending the Wall.
- **Location:** Tucked into a small alcove hidden behind a loose brick.

By successfully finding and deciphering these clues, players can gain significant advantages as they navigate the Crumbling Section and other dangers of the Wall.

Encounter with the Dune Drakes

Two Dune Drakes use this section as a nesting area. They are fiercely territorial and will attack any intruders.

Dune Drake Attack

Flyby Attack: The Dune Drakes will use their Flyby ability to swoop in, attack, and retreat without provoking opportunity attacks. They will coordinate their attacks, focusing on isolated or injured PCs.

Fire Breath: Once per encounter, each drake will use its Fire Breath, forcing the characters to make a DC 13 Dexterity saving throw or take 24 (7d6) fire damage.

Player Response:

Combat: PCs must fend off the drakes while also dealing with the unstable terrain. Utilize strategic positioning and teamwork to overcome the drakes.

Diplomacy (Unlikely): If any characters speak Draconic and attempt to communicate, a high DC 20 Charisma (Persuasion) check might convince the Dune Drakes to allow them to pass without further conflict.

Terrain

Unstable Wall Section: Movement speed is halved due to the risk of falling debris and unstable footing. Characters must succeed on a DC 15 Dexterity (Athletics or Acrobatics) check every 10 feet they move or at regular intervals at the DM's discretion. Failing this check results in falling 20 feet and taking 1d6 bludgeoning damage.

Falling Debris: At the start of each PC's turn, they must make a DC 12 Dexterity saving throw to avoid falling debris. On a failed save, they take 2d6 bludgeoning damage and fall 20 feet.

Lair Actions

On initiative count 20 (losing initiative ties), the Crumbling Section invokes one of the following lair actions:

Rockslide: Large chunks of the Wall break loose and fall. Each creature in a 20-foot radius must make a DC

14 Dexterity saving throw or take 3d6 bludgeoning damage and fall 20 feet.

Blinding Dust: A cloud of dust rises, obscuring vision. All creatures in a 30-foot radius must succeed on a DC 13 Constitution saving throw or be blinded until the end of their next turn.

Crack Expansion: A large crack suddenly widens, creating difficult terrain in a 10-foot radius. Any creature in this area must make a DC 14 Dexterity saving throw or fall 20 feet, taking 2d6 bludgeoning damage.

Scaling the Encounter

Beginning Players (PC levels 1-5)

- Reduce the number of Dune Drakes.
- Lower the DCs for skill checks and saves.
- Simplify lair actions and reduce damage output.

Intermediate Players (PC levels 6-10)

- Use standard encounter setups as described.
- Maintain original DCs and damage for skill checks and environmental hazards.

Advanced Players (PC levels 11+)

- Increase the number and strength of Dune Drakes.
- Raise the DCs for skill checks and saves.
- Enhance lair actions and increase damage output.

Monster

Dune Drake (2)

The Old Security Gate

The party encounters an ancient, rusted gate with remnants of old-world security systems that still pose a threat. They must navigate through Advanced Security Drones, a laser grid, and logic puzzles to bypass the gate's control systems.

This gate leads to a 100-foot tunnel that cuts through the Wall, providing a shortcut if successfully navigated.

The security systems are arranged in layers:

- Two Advanced Security Drones patrol the airspace around the platform, 20 feet above it.
- A laser grid covers the gate entrance, visible as faint red beams.
- The control panel for the gate, containing logic puzzles, is located next to the gate itself.

As you continue to climb the vast face of the Wall, you come to a large platform cut into the Wall itself, upon which an ancient, rusted gate looms before you, a relic of the old world. The gate is heavily fortified, with faded warnings and old world insignia barely visible through layers of rust and grime. This once-imposing structure is now a crumbling monument to a lost era, but its purpose is still clear: to keep intruders out.

Beyond the gate, you can see a dark tunnel cutting directly through the Wall, stretching into the unknown. The air is thick with the scent of ozone and decay, a stark reminder of the dangers that lie ahead.

As you approach the platform, you notice two spherical objects hovering about 20 feet above it. They appear to be some kind of automated drones, their metallic surfaces gleaming in the harsh light. A soft buzzing emanates from them as they patrol in a regular pattern.

Closer to the gate itself, you see faint red beams crisscrossing the entrance, forming a complex grid. Occasional sparks dance along these beams, hinting at their deadly nature.

To the right of the gate, a control panel blinks with dim, flickering lights, its surface covered in ancient symbols and what appear to be complex locking mechanisms.

Activities

Disable Security Systems: PCs must either use Technology checks to disable the Advanced Security Drones and laser grid, find a way to bypass the security systems, or simply fight their way through.

Solve Logic Puzzles: Players encounter a series of logic puzzles to bypass the Security Gate's control systems. Success opens the gate, while failure triggers additional security measures.

Navigate the Tunnel: Once inside, PCs must navigate the 100-foot tunnel, dealing with any residual security measures and traps.

Disable Security Systems

PCs can use their skills in Technology to disable the ancient security systems that still guard the Old Security Gate. This involves deactivating the Advanced Security Drones and bypassing the deadly laser grid. Alternatively, the party can enter into battle with the drones and destroy the laser grid, or even use other

creative methods to bypass them altogether. Success in this activity allows the party to safely traverse the gate and the tunnel beyond, while failure triggers additional security measures and potential combat encounters.

Skill Checks and Steps

Assess the Situation

Check: PCs may make a DC 13 Intelligence (Technology) check to assess each new security system and identify the best approach to disable it.

Success: Characters gain advantage on their next check to disable either the drones or the laser grid.

Failure: Characters must proceed without the advantage, and any failure in subsequent checks triggers an immediate security response.

Disable Advanced Security Drones

Check: Depending on their approach, PCs can make either an Intelligence (Technology) check using engineer's tools OR a Dexterity (Technology) check using thieves' tools (DC 15 each) to disable the Advanced Security Drones.

Success: Successfully disabling a drone prevents it from activating and attacking the PCs. Each successful check disables one drone.

Failure: The Advanced Security Drone activates and attacks the nearest character. Combat ensues with the drone using its Laser Beam and Taser Shock abilities.

Bypass Laser Grid

Check: PCs must make a DC 15 Dexterity (Technology) check using engineer's tools or thieves' tools to temporarily disable or bypass the laser grid. Two total checks are needed, one for each section of the grid.

Success: Successfully bypassing the laser grid allows the party to move through the area without triggering the security lasers. Two successful checks are needed for a total Success to bypass the grid. Each successful check temporarily disables one section of the grid.

Failure: The entire laser grid activates and moves its lasers to cross in front of the control panel, requiring all creatures within 10 feet to make a DC 15 Dexterity saving throw or take 3d6 fire damage.

Backup Systems

Check: Once the primary systems are disabled, PCs must deal with backup systems. This requires a DC 16 Intelligence (Investigation) or Wisdom (Perception) check to locate, and a DC 16 Intelligence (Technology) check to deactivate the hidden failsafes.

Success: Disables the backup systems, preventing additional security measures from activating.

Failure: Triggers a secondary alarm, summoning additional Advanced Security Drones.

Timing Mechanism

Check: PCs have a limited amount of time before the security systems reset. Each attempt to disable a system must be completed within 1 minute. If PCs fail to disable the system in time, they must start over.

Success: Characters manage to disable the systems within the time limit.

Failure: The system resets, andPCs must deal with any activated drones or laser grid sections.

Possible Outcomes

Complete Success

- PCs disable all security systems without triggering any alarms or combat encounters.
- They gain safe passage through the gate and tunnel, avoiding unnecessary risks.

Partial Success

- PCs disable some but not all security systems. They may encounter a few activated Advanced Security Drones or the laser grid but manage to deal with them efficiently.
- They gain passage through the gate and tunnel but face some hazards.

Failure

- PCs fail to disable or otherwise bypass the security

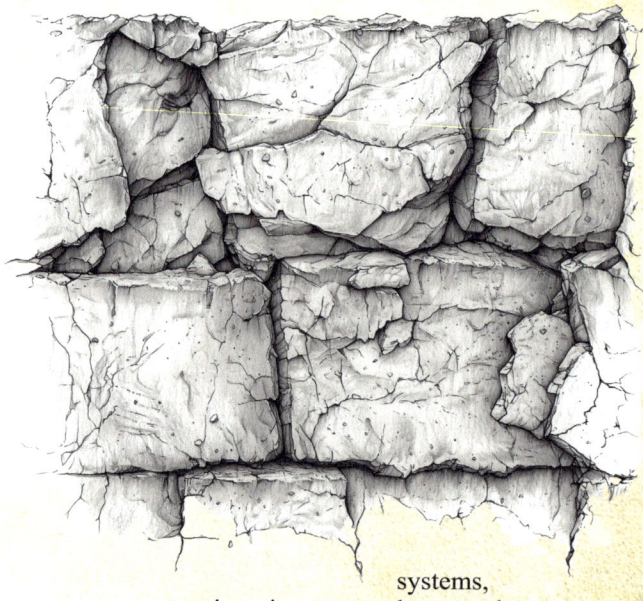

systems, triggering alarms and combat encounters with multiple Advanced Security Drones and the active laser grid.

- Passage through the gate and tunnel becomes a dangerous endeavor, requiring additional skill checks and combat.

Solve Logic Puzzles

The party encounters a series of three logic puzzles embedded within the Security Gate's control systems. These puzzles are designed to test different aspects of problem-solving and must be completed in sequence to fully bypass the gate's security measures.

DMs are encouraged to use one, two, or all three logic puzzles to challenge their players, depending on the desired difficulty level and time constraints. This decision is entirely up to DM discretion.

- **Light Grid Puzzle**: Solving this deactivates the outer laser grid.

- **Mechanical Gears and Levers Puzzle**: Completing this disables the Advanced Security Drones.

- **Memory Sequence Puzzle**: Solving the final puzzle unlocks the Security Gate.

Successfully solving each puzzle deactivates a layer of security. Completing all three puzzles allows the party to fully bypass the gate's defenses and open the Security Gate. Failure to solve a puzzle may trigger additional security measures, such as activating more Advanced Security Drones or reinforcing the remaining security layers.

If the DM chooses to use fewer puzzles, adjust the outcomes accordingly:

- **Using one puzzle**: Solving it opens the gate directly.

- **Using two puzzles**: The first disables defenses, the second opens the gate.

Light Grid Puzzle

The PCs encounter a grid of lights embedded in a control panel. The goal is to turn off all the lights by pressing them. When a character presses a light, it toggles the state of that light (on or off) as well as its adjacent lights (those up, down, left, and right of the pressed light). The puzzle requires players to figure out the correct sequence of presses to turn off all the lights.

Setup

- Draw a 3x3 grid (or any size you prefer) on a piece of paper or a whiteboard. Mark the initial state of each light (on or off). For simplicity, start with all lights turned on.

Initial Setup Example (3x3 Grid)

1	1	1
1	1	1
1	1	1

Instructions for Players

"Before you is a control panel with a grid of lights, all of them clearly lit up (or 'on'). Your goal is to turn off all the lights by pressing them. When you press a light, it will toggle its state (on or off) as well as the state of the lights adjacent to it (up, down, left, and right of the pressed light)."

"For example, if you press the light in the center, it will toggle itself and the lights directly above, below, to the left, and to the right of it."

"Think carefully about your moves, as each press affects multiple lights. You must figure out the sequence of presses needed to turn off all the lights."

Gameplay

Allow the players to discuss and decide which light to press.

When a player decides to press a light, update the grid accordingly:

- Toggle the state of the pressed light.
- Toggle the state of the adjacent lights (up, down, left, and right).
- Update the grid and show the players the new state of the lights.

Continue this process until the players turn off all the lights or they decide to reset and try a new strategy.

Example Steps to Solve the Puzzle

1) Players press the center light (B2):

	A	B	C
1	1	0	1
2	0	0	0
3	1	0	1

2) Players press the top-left light (A1):

	A	B	C
1	0	1	1
2	1	0	0
3	1	0	1

3) Players press the top-right light (C1):

	A	B	C
1	0	0	0
2	1	0	1
3	1	0	1

4) Players press the bottom-right light (C3):

	A	B	C
1	0	0	0
2	1	0	0
3	1	1	0

5) Finally, players press the bottom-left light (A3):

	A	B	C
1	0	0	0
2	0	0	0
3	0	0	0

Success

Once all the lights are turned off, the gate's outer security system recognizes the solution and deactivates the laser grid. This allows the party to proceed to the next security layer.

If using multiple puzzles: The party must now face the next puzzle (Mechanical Gears and Levers) to continue disabling the security measures.

If using only this puzzle: The gate fully unlocks, allowing the party to proceed through the Security Gate and the tunnel beyond.

DM Note: This puzzle is the first of three potential security layers. DMs are encouraged to use one, two, or all three logic puzzles to challenge their players, depending on the desired difficulty level and time constraints. This decision is entirely up to DM discretion. If using fewer puzzles, adjust the outcomes so that completing the final chosen puzzle fully unlocks the gate.

Failure

If the players struggle to solve the puzzle and make multiple unsuccessful attempts, they may trigger additional security measures. For example, after a certain number of failed attempts (determined by the DM), another Advanced Security Drone might activate, or the laser grid may intensify.

Mechanical Gears and Levers Puzzle

Gear Configuration

Gears A, B, and C form a triangle where C is at the apex.

Gears D and E are below this triangle, with Gear C also acting as a central pivot point or connection between the upper triangle and these two gears. However, D and E are not directly connected to each other; they connect only through C.

Levers

Lever 1 affects gears A and B, allowing them to rotate together or in opposition.

Lever 2 controls gear C, which in turn can move all other gears due to its central position.

Lever 3 independently adjusts gears D and E.

Instructions for the DM

Visual Aid: Create a diagram or use a physical prop showing this setup. You can draw circles for gears and lines for connections, labeling them as described.

Mechanism Description for Players: "You see a complex mechanism with five gears arranged in a pattern. Gears A, B, and C form a triangle at the top, with C at the peak. Below, gears D and E are positioned such that they can interact with C but not directly with each other. Three levers are present; each controls different parts of this mechanism."

Objective

Players must manipulate the levers to align all gears in a specific manner (perhaps all gears need to rotate to a point where a hidden mechanism clicks, or lights align, etc.).

Lever Functions

Lever 1: Moves gears A and B. When pulled, A rotates clockwise, and B counterclockwise, or vice versa.

Lever 2: Rotates gear C. This movement will affect all connected gears (A, B, D, E).

Lever 3: Moves gears D and E independently of each other but through their connection with C.

Additional Tips for the DM

Demonstration: If possible, demonstrate how one lever affects the gears to give players a starting point.

Puzzle Solution: Decide on a sequence or final position for the gears. For example, all gears might need to have a marked tooth pointing upwards or in a particular direction to unlock the mechanism.

Instructions for Players

- "Before you is a complex mechanism of interlocking gears and levers. Your task is to align the gears in the correct configuration to disengage the lock mechanism and open the gate."

- "Each lever affects certain gears. Lever 1 affects Gears A and D, Lever 2 affects Gears B and E, and Lever 3 affects Gears C and D."

- "You must manipulate the levers and gears carefully and in the correct order to achieve the correct alignment."

Gameplay

Identify the Gears and Levers:

- **Check:** Each PC must make a DC 13 Intelligence (Investigation or Technology) check to understand how the gears and levers interact.

- **Success:** PCs gain insight into the mechanism and have advantage on their next check to manipulate the gears.

- **Failure:** PCs do not gain additional insight but can still attempt to manipulate the gears.

Manipulate the Gears:

- **Check:** PCs must make a separate DC 15 Intelligence (Technology) check to determine the correct order to manipulate the gears and levers.

- **Solution:** Players must adjust the levers in the correct sequence to align the gears. For example:

  - Pull Lever 1 (aligns Gear A and D)

  - Pull Lever 2 (aligns Gear B and E)

  - Pull Lever 3 (aligns Gear C and D)

Solution Steps

- PCs pull Lever 1, which aligns Gear A with Gear D.
- PCs pull Lever 2, which aligns Gear B with Gear E.
- PCs pull Lever 3, which aligns Gear C with Gear D.

Success

If the party successfully aligns the gears in the correct order, the gate's control system recognizes the correct alignment order and deactivates the Advanced Security Drones. This allows the party to proceed to the final security layer to fully unlock the gate.

Failure

If the party fails the check and manipulates the gears in the incorrect order, a trap is activated. Describe the trap's activation and effects:

Disabling Gas Trap

Description: The mechanism releases a cloud of disabling gas into the area.

Trigger: Failing to align the gears in the correct order (failing the check).

Activation: The trap activates immediately upon failure.

Effect: All creatures in the area must make a DC 13 Constitution saving throw or be poisoned for 1 hour.

Detection: PCs can make a DC 15 Wisdom (Perception) check to notice faint hissing sounds or gas vents the moment they misalign the gears.

Disable: PCs can make a DC 15 Dexterity check using thieves' tools to disable the gas vents if they detect the trap.

Memory Sequence Puzzle

Puzzle Description: The party encounters a control panel that displays a sequence of lights and sounds. The goal is to repeat the sequence correctly to bypass the gate's security system. The sequence becomes progressively more complex, requiring players or their characters to use their memory and attention to detail.

Instructions for the DM

Prepare a series of light and sound sequences (start with 3-4 steps and increase the complexity with each round). You can use a visual/audio aid or describe the lights and sounds.

Describe the panel to the players and explain that they need to repeat the sequence to unlock the gate. This can either be performed by the characters using skill checks, or by the players themselves using their own memory skills.

Example Sequence

Round 1: Red light, blue light, beep

Round 2: Red light, blue light, beep, green light

Round 3: Red light, blue light, beep, green light, buzz

Round 4: Red light, blue light, beep, green light, buzz, yellow light

Instructions for Players

"Before you is a control panel with several colored lights and speakers. To bypass the gate's security system, you need to observe the sequence of lights and sounds and then repeat it correctly. If you wish, you may designate one character or player to perform the checks and solve the puzzle."

"The panel will display a sequence. Pay close attention to the order of the lights and sounds."

"You must repeat the sequence exactly as it was shown. If you make a mistake, the system will activate additional security measures."

Gameplay Using Skill Checks

Observe the Sequence

- **Check:** One or more PCs must make a DC 15 Intelligence (Investigation) or Wisdom (Perception) check to observe the sequence of lights and sounds.
- **Success:** PCs successfully observe the sequence and gain advantage on the next check to repeat it.
- **Failure:** PCs still observe the sequence but do not gain advantage.

Repeat the Sequence

- **Check:** One or more PCs must make a DC 15 Intelligence (Investigation) check to recall the sequence correctly.
- **Solution:** PCs must correctly recall and replicate the sequence of lights and sounds in the right order.
  - For example: If the sequence was Red light, blue light, beep, green light,PCs must repeat: Red light, blue light, beep, green light.

Example Steps to Solve the Puzzle

- DM: "The panel displays the following sequence: Red light, blue light, beep, green light. Observe carefully."
- One or more PCs make their checks:
  - PC 1: DC 15 Intelligence (Investigation) check to observe. Success, gains advantage.
  - PC 2: DC 15 Wisdom (Perception) check to observe. Failure, does not gain advantage.
- DM: "Now, repeat the sequence."
  - Player 1 repeats the sequence: Red light, blue light, beep, green light.
  - Player 2 repeats the sequence: Red light, blue light, beep, green light.

- If players or their characters successfully repeat the sequence, they move to the next round with an additional step added.

Success

If players successfully repeat the sequence correctly for all rounds, the gate's security system recognizes the solution and allows the PCs to unlock the Security Gate, granting access to the tunnel beyond.

Navigate the Tunnel

Once inside the Old Security Gate, the party must navigate a 100-foot tunnel that cuts through the Wall. The tunnel is filled with residual security measures and traps that the PCs must identify and disable or avoid to safely reach the other side.

Detecting Security Measures and Traps

Check: PCs must make a DC 15 Wisdom (Perception) or Intelligence (Investigation) check to detect traps and security measures.

Success: PCs identify the traps and security measures before triggering them.

Failure: PCs do not detect the traps and may trigger them, causing adverse effects.

Navigating the Tunnel

Check: PCs must make a series of skill checks to navigate the tunnel without triggering the security measures.

Solution: PCs need to carefully navigate the tunnel, disabling traps or avoiding them using their skills.

Traps and Security Measures

Floor Panel Trap

Description: A pressure-sensitive panel in the floor triggers spikes to shoot up from the ground.

Trigger: Stepping on the panel.

Effect: DC 13 Dexterity saving throw or take 2d6 piercing damage.

Detection: DC 15 Wisdom (Perception) check to notice the slightly raised panel.

Disable: DC 15 Dexterity check using thieves' tools to disable the panel mechanism.

Security Drone

Description: A drone equipped with laser beams and taser shocks patrols the tunnel.

Trigger: Detects movement within 30 feet.

Effect: Laser Beam: *Ranged Weapon Attack:* +4 to hit, range 60 ft., one target. *Hit:* 7 (1d8 + 2) fire damage. Taser Shock: *Melee Weapon Attack:* +4 to hit, reach 5 ft., one target. *Hit:* 5 (1d6 + 2) lightning damage and the target must succeed on a DC 13 Constitution saving throw or be stunned until the end of its next turn.

Detection: DC 15 Intelligence (Investigation) or Wisdom (Perception) check to notice the hidden drone.

Disable: DC 15 Dexterity (Stealth) check to sneak past the drone, or DC 15 Intelligence (Technology) check to deactivate the drone without alerting it.

Laser Grid

Description: A grid of laser beams blocks the tunnel, triggered by movement.

Trigger: Passing through the grid without deactivation.

Effect: DC 13 Dexterity saving throw or take 3d6 fire damage.

Detection: DC 15 Wisdom (Perception) check to notice the faint laser lines.

Disable: DC 15 Dexterity (Technology) check using engineer's tools or thieves' tools to deactivate the laser grid controls.

Terrain

Rusted Metal and Concrete: The ground is uneven and covered with debris from the deteriorating structure. Movement speed is halved, and PCs must make a DC 12 Dexterity (Acrobatics) check every 20 feet to avoid tripping or slipping.

Laser Grids: The laser grids require careful navigation. PCs must make a DC 15 Dexterity saving throw to avoid taking 3d6 fire damage from the lasers.

Lair Actions

On initiative count 20 (losing initiative ties), the Old Security Gate invokes one of the following lair actions:

Drone Activation: An additional Advanced Security Drone activates and attacks the nearest PC.

Laser Surge: The laser grids momentarily intensify. All creatures within 10 feet of the grid must make a DC 15 Dexterity saving throw or take 3d6 fire damage.

Security Lockdown: The gate's control systems initiate a lockdown. PCs must succeed on a DC 15 Intelligence (Technology) check to prevent the gate from sealing shut for 1 minute.

Scaling the Encounter

Beginning Players (PC levels 1-5)

General Adjustments

- Reduce the number of Advanced Security Drones.

- Lower the DCs for skill checks and saves.

- Simplify lair actions and reduce damage output.

Specific Adjustments

Disable Security Systems

- **Assess the Situation**: DC 10 Intelligence (Technology) check.

- **Disable Advanced Security Drones**: DC 12 Technology check.

- **Drone Attacks (Reduced):** Laser Beam (+2 to hit, 1d6 fire damage) and Taser Shock (+2 to hit, 1d4 lightning damage, DC 10 Constitution save to avoid stun).

- **Bypass Laser Grids**: DC 12 Dexterity (Technology) check using engineer's tools or thieves' tools.

- Failing check results in DC 12 Dexterity save to avoid 2d6 fire damage.

- **Backup Systems**: DC 13 Intelligence (Investigation) or Wisdom (Perception) check, DC 13 Intelligence (Technology) check.

- Failure summons 1 Advanced Security Drone.

Solve Logic Puzzles

- Reduce the complexity of the light grid and gear puzzles.

- Allow more time for memory sequence puzzle attempts.

Navigate the Tunnel

- **Detecting and Avoiding Security Measures and Traps**: DC radiant 12 Wisdom (Perception) or Intelligence (Investigation) checks, DC 12 Dexterity (Stealth) or Intelligence (Technology) checks.

- **Reduce Damage from Traps**:

  - **Floor Panel Trap**: DC 10 Dexterity save, 1d6 piercing damage.

  - **Advanced Security Drone**: Laser Beam (+2 to hit, 1d6 fire damage), Taser Shock (+2 to hit, 1d4 lightning damage).

  - **Laser Grid**: DC 12 Dexterity save, 2d6 fire damage.

Lair Actions

- **Drone Activation**: 1 additional Advanced Security Drone with reduced stats.

- **Laser Surge**: DC 12 Dexterity save, 2d6 fire damage.

- **Security Lockdown**: DC 12 Intelligence (Technology) check to prevent gate from sealing.

Intermediate Players (PC levels 6-10)

General Adjustments

- Use standard encounter setups as described.

- Maintain original DCs and damage for skill checks and environmental hazards.

Specific Adjustments

Disable Security Systems

- **Assess the Situation**: DC 13 Intelligence (Technology) check.

- **Disable Advanced Security Drones**: DC 15 Technology check.

- **Drone Attacks (Standard)**: Laser Beam (+4 to hit, 1d8+2 fire damage) and Taser Shock (+4 to hit, 1d6+2 lightning damage, DC 13 Constitution save to avoid stun).

- **Bypass Laser Grids**: DC 15 Dexterity (Technology) check using engineer's tools or thieves' tools.

- Failing check results in DC 15 Dexterity save to avoid 3d6 fire damage.

- **Backup Systems**: DC 16 Intelligence (Investigation) or Wisdom (Perception) check, DC 16 Intelligence (Technology) check.

- Failure summons 1d4 Advanced Security Drones.

Solve Logic Puzzles

- Standard complexity for light grid, gear puzzles, and memory sequence puzzle.

Navigate the Tunnel

- **Detecting and Avoiding Security Measures and Traps**: DC 15 Wisdom (Perception) or Intelligence (Investigation) checks, DC 15 Dexterity (Stealth) or Intelligence (Technology) checks.

- **Standard Trap Damage**:

  - **Floor Panel Trap**: DC 13 Dexterity save, 2d6 piercing damage.

  - **Advanced Security Drone**: Laser Beam (+4 to hit, 1d8+2 fire damage), Taser Shock (+4 to hit, 1d6+2 lightning damage).

  - **Laser Grid**: DC 15 Dexterity save, 3d6 fire damage.

Lair Actions

Drone Activation: 1d4 Advanced Security Drones with standard stats.

Laser Surge: DC 15 Dexterity save, 3d6 fire damage.

Security Lockdown: DC 15 Intelligence (Technology) check to prevent gate from sealing.

Advanced Players (PC levels 11+)

General Adjustments

- Increase the number and strength of Advanced Security Drones.
- Raise the DCs for skill checks and saves.
- Enhance lair actions and increase damage output.

Specific Adjustments

Disable Security Systems

- **Assess the Situation**: DC 16 Intelligence (Technology) check.
- **Disable Advanced Security Drones**: DC 18 Technology check.
- **Drone Attacks (Enhanced)**: Laser Beam (+6 to hit, 2d8+3 fire damage) and Taser Shock (+6 to hit, 2d6+3 lightning damage, DC 16 Constitution save to avoid stun).
- **Bypass Laser Grids**: DC 18 Dexterity (Technology) check using engineer's tools or thieves' tools.
- Failing check results in DC 18 Dexterity save to avoid 4d6 fire damage.
- **Backup Systems**: DC 19 Intelligence (Investigation) or Wisdom (Perception) check and DC 19 Intelligence (Technology check).

- Failure summons 1d6 Advanced Security Drones.

Solve Logic Puzzles

- Increase the complexity and number of steps for light grid, gear puzzles, and memory sequence puzzle.

Navigate the Tunnel

- **Detecting and Avoiding Security Measures and Traps**: DC 18 Wisdom (Perception) or Intelligence (Investigation) checks, DC 18 Dexterity (Stealth) or Intelligence (Technology) checks.
- **Enhanced Trap Damage**:
  - **Floor Panel Trap**: DC 16 Dexterity save, 3d6 piercing damage.
  - **Advanced Security Drone**: Laser Beam (+6 to hit, 2d8+3 fire damage), Taser Shock (+6 to hit, 2d6+3 lightning damage).
  - **Laser Grid**: DC 18 Dexterity save, 4d6 fire damage.

Lair Actions

- **Drone Activation**: 1d6 Advanced Security Drones with enhanced stats.
- **Laser Surge**: DC 18 Dexterity save, 4d6 fire damage.
- **Security Lockdown**: DC 18 Intelligence (Technology) check to prevent gate from sealing.

Monster

Advanced Security Drone (2-4)

The Hidden Armory

The players discover a concealed chamber within the Wall that contains valuable old-world weapons and gear. They must navigate traps and defeat automated defenses to access the Armory's contents. Techno-Ghosts provide clues about the Lifeline Pipeline and the water source near Hope Falls.

As you continue to ascend the Wall's sheer surface, you come upon a platform cut into the face of the Wall. Once you clear away the rubble, you uncover a hidden entrance leading into a dimly lit chamber. The air inside is cool and heavy with the scent of rust and old machinery. Rows of weapon racks and storage lockers line the walls, filled with the remnants of pre-apocalypse technology. Faint blue lights flicker intermittently, casting eerie shadows across the room.

Amid the silence, you hear the soft hum of dormant machinery, and the occasional crackle of static electricity. The walls are adorned with fading schematics and maintenance logs, remnants of a time when this armory was a bustling hub of activity. It's clear that the technology within these walls, though aged, holds the potential to significantly aid your mission.

Activities

Disable Traps: PCs must use their skills to identify and disable pressure-sensitive floor tiles.

Solve Puzzles: PCs encounter a series of riddles and complex locking mechanisms to access the Armory's contents.

Combat Defenses: PCs must fight off Advanced Security Drones and turret guns.

Interact with Techno-Ghosts: Obtain vital information about the Lifeline Pipeline and the old water source.

The following activities must be completed in the exact order as listed because the floor tile traps must be disabled first to ensure safe movement within the Armory.

• Detect and Disable Floor Tile Traps

• Solve the Riddle Puzzle

• Solve the Complex Locking Mechanism

Solving the riddle puzzle and the complex locking mechanism sequentially are essential to unlocking the vault and accessing its contents, while any deviation could trigger additional security measures and hinder progress.

Disable Traps

PCs encounter pressure-sensitive floor tiles that trigger traps if stepped on incorrectly. They must identify and disable these traps to proceed safely.

Detecting the Traps

Check: PCs must make a DC 15 Wisdom (Perception) check to identify pressure-sensitive floor tiles.

Success: PCs notice the slightly raised tiles and avoid triggering the traps.

Failure: PCs do not notice the traps and risk activating them.

Disabling the Traps

Check: PCs must make a DC 15 Dexterity check using thieves' tools to disable the trap mechanism.

Success: The trap is disabled safely.

Failure: The trap activates, releasing a cloud of disabling gas.

Trap Effects

Trigger: Stepping on a pressure-sensitive tile or failing to disable the trap.

Effect: The trap releases a cloud of disabling gas. All characters within a 10-foot radius must make a DC 13 Constitution saving throw or be poisoned for 1 hour.

Solve Puzzles

Players encounter a series of riddles and complex locking mechanisms that guard the Armory's most valuable contents. They must solve these puzzles to access the gear inside.

Riddle Puzzle

Puzzle: A panel displays a riddle that must be solved to unlock a storage locker.

Riddle Example: "I speak without a mouth and hear without ears. I have no body, but I come alive with wind. What am I?"

Solution: An echo.

Check: PCs must make a DC 15 Intelligence check to solve the riddle.

Success: The locker opens, revealing valuable equipment.

Failure: The locker remains locked, and a minor trap is triggered, such as a dart trap requiring a DC 13 Dexterity saving throw to avoid 2d4 piercing damage.

Additional Riddles

Riddle: "I am the legacy of ancient times, a whisper of the past. Stored in fragments of metal and glass, my knowledge unsurpassed. What am I?" **Answer:** Data

Riddle: "I am a silent guardian, always watching, never sleeping. My gaze sees all, through walls and ceilings, never weeping. What am I?" **Answer:** Security Camera

Riddle: "With eyes that see the unseen and hands that touch the untouchable, I move without a sound and leave no trace. What am I?" **Answer:** Ghost

Riddle: "What loses its head in the morning and gains it back at night?" **Answer:** Pillow

Riddle: "I am born from decay, yet I bring forth new life. In the remnants of the old world, I thrive. What am I?" **Answer:** Fungi

Complex Locking Mechanism

Puzzle: A series of gears and levers must be aligned to disengage a lock.

Check: PCs must make a DC 15 Dexterity check using engineer's tools or thieves' tools to adjust the gears in the correct order.

Success: The mechanism unlocks, granting access to a weapons cache.

Failure: The mechanism jams, and an Advanced Security Drone activates, attacking the party.

Encounter with Techno-Ghosts

Description: PCs encounter Techno-Ghosts, spectral remnants of old-world security systems in the Armory. These entities guard the Armory and possess valuable information. The Techno-Ghosts can appear at any time.

Techno-Ghost Dialogue: The Techno-Ghost provides clues about the Lifeline Pipeline and the water source.

Combat Initiation: If PCs fail to communicate effectively or threaten the Techno-Ghost, it attacks.

Techno-Ghost Clues:

- **Pipeline Connection:** "The Lifeline Pipeline connects to large underground pools located beyond the Wall. You must restore its function to transport water."

- **Unlocking Secrets:** "To unlock the Armory's true potential, you must find the hidden panels, align the gears, and bypass the security protocols."

- **Pumps Needed**: "To restore the water flow, you will need powerful pumps to propel the groundwater through the ancient pipelines."

- **Parts in Urban Ruins**: "The parts required to repair the pumps may be found in the ruins of urban environments."

- **Beware of Mutants**: "The lands beyond the Wall are infested with mutants. Beware of their vicious attacks."

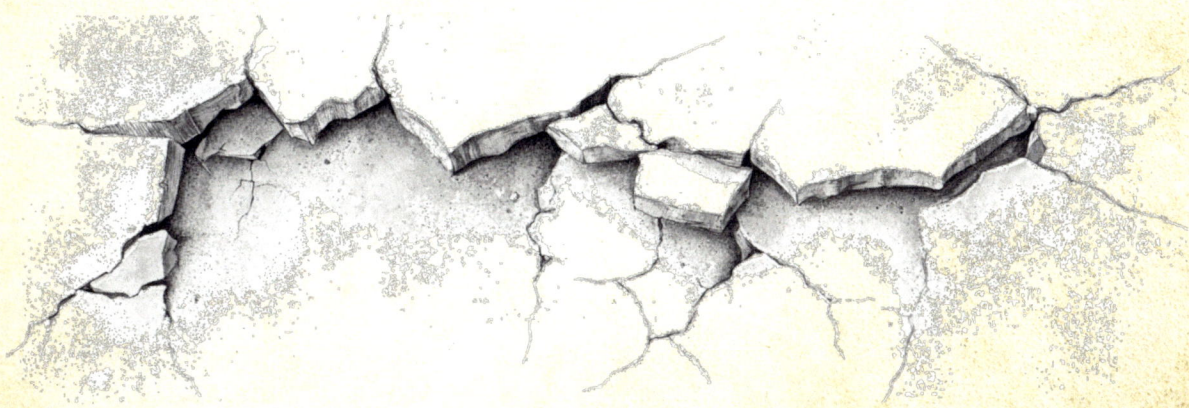

Armory Table

Name	Description	Damage	Properties	Weight	Damaged Check
Plasma Rifle	An old-world energy weapon that emits a concentrated plasma bolt.	2d10 fire damage	Range 60/240 ft., Two-Handed, Recharge 1d4 rounds	8 lbs	DC 15 Intelligence (Technology) check tooperate it correctly. If failed, the rifle misfires and needs repair.
Shock Baton	A metal baton that delivers an electric shock on impact.	1d8 lightning damage	Light, Finesse, Melee Weapon, Stuns target for 1 round on critical hit (DC 13 Constitution saving throw)	2 lbs	DC 12 Intelligence (Technology) check. If failed, the baton shorts out and does not deliver the shock.
Energy Shield	A collapsible shield that projects a small energy barrier.	+2 AC	Requires attunement, grants advantage on Dexterity saving throws against ranged attacks	6 lbs	DC 14 Intelligence (Technology) check. If failed, the shield's energy field flickers and does not provide full protection.
Laser Pistol	A small handgun that fires precise laser beams.	1d8 fire damage	Range 40/120 ft., Light, Recharge 1d6 rounds	3 lbs	DC 13 Intelligence (Technology) check. If failed, the pistol's targeting system malfunctions, causing disadvantage on attacks.
Tactical Helmet	A helmet equipped with a heads-up display and targeting systems.	+1 AC	Grants darkvision 60 ft., advantage on Wisdom (Perception) checks	5 lbs	DC 12 Intelligence (Technology) check. If failed, the display glitches, providing no bonus to Perception.
Cryo Grenade	A grenade that releases a burst of freezing energy upon detonation.	3d6 cold damage (10 ft. radius)	Range 20/60 ft., Freezes targets in place for 1 round (DC 14 Constitution saving throw)	1 lb	DC 15 Intelligence (Technology) check. If failed, the grenade fails to detonate properly.
Auto-Turret	A portable turret that can be set up to provide covering fire.	1d6 piercing damage per round	Range 80/320 ft., Automated targeting, Requires Intelligence (Technology) check to deploy (DC 14)	12 lbs	DC 14 Intelligence (Technology) check. If failed, the turret jams and does not fire.
Power Armor	A suit of mechanized armor that enhances strength and durability.	N/A	Grants +2 Strength, +2 AC, Resistance to bludgeoning, piercing, and slashing damage	45 lbs	DC 17 Intelligence (Technology) check. If failed, the armor's servos malfunction, reducing movement speed by 10 ft.
Sonic Disruptor	A handheld device that emits a powerful sonic wave.	2d6 thunder damage	Range 30/90 ft., Disorients targets (DC 14 Constitution saving throw)	4 lbs	DC 13 Intelligence (Technology) check. If failed, the disruptor's frequency is off, reducing damage to 1d6.
Grav Boots	Boots that allow the wearer to manipulate gravity and jump great distances.	N/A	Grants jump distance triple the normal, advantage on Athletics or Acrobatics checks involving jumping.	3 lbs	DC 14 Intelligence (Technology) check. If failed, the boots' grav modules misfire, causing the wearer to fall prone.

Terrain

The Hidden Armory is a cluttered and confined space filled with old-world technology. The terrain includes:

Obstructed Paths: Narrow aisles and debris-covered floors. Movement speed is reduced by half unless a DC 12 Dexterity (Athletics or Acrobatics) check is made.

Pressure-Sensitive Floor Tiles: Hidden traps that can be detected with a DC 15 Wisdom (Perception) check and disabled with a DC 15 Dexterity check using thieves' tools. If triggered, a trap releases a cloud of disabling gas, requiring a DC 13 Constitution saving throw to avoid being poisoned for 1 hour.

Static Interference: Electronic devices have a 20% chance of malfunctioning each round they are used in the Armory.

Lair Actions

Security System Activation (Initiative Count 20 - Losing Ties): The security system activates, releasing an electromagnetic pulse. All electronic devices and constructs in the room must make a DC 13 Constitution saving throw or be stunned for 1 minute.

Turret Gun Deployment (Initiative Count 10): Hidden turret guns emerge from the walls and target the PCs. Each turret makes one ranged attack with a +5 to hit, dealing 8 (1d10 + 3) piercing damage on a hit.

Reinforcement Drones (Initiative Count 5): Two Advanced Security Drones activate and join the battle.

Scaling the Encounter

Beginning Players (PC levels 1-5)

- Reduce the number of traps and enemies.
- Lower the DCs for skill checks and saves.
- Simplify puzzles and reduce damage output.

Intermediate Players (PC levels 6-10)

- Use standard encounter setups as described.
- Maintain original DCs and damage for skill checks and environmental hazards.

Advanced Players (PC levels 11+)

- Increase the number and strength of traps and enemies.
- Raise the DCs for skill checks and saves.
- Enhance puzzles and increase damage output.

Monsters

Advanced Security Drone

Techno-Ghost (1-2)

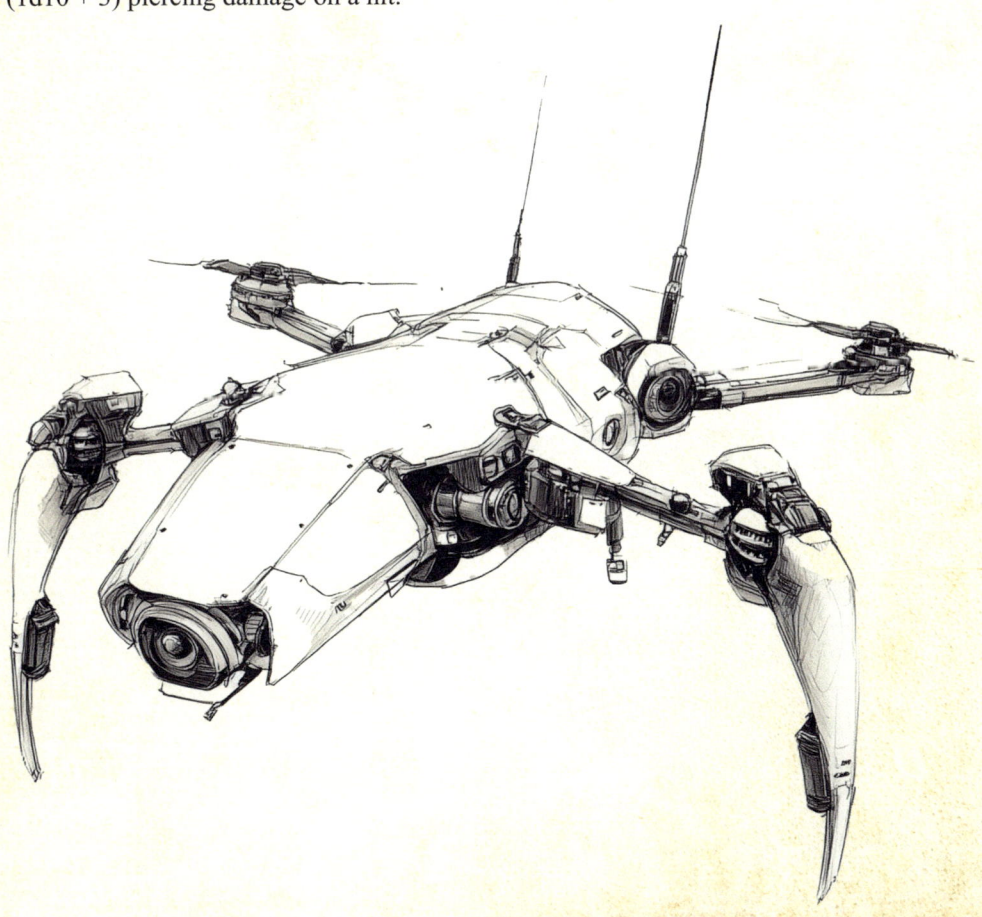

The Guardian's Perch

This high vantage point atop the Wall offers a panoramic view of the surrounding Wasteland and the Wall itself, providing strategic insights for the players. Skywatcher Finn, a reclusive scout with valuable information about the terrain and dangers beyond the Wall, can be persuaded to assist the PCs.

As you reach the top of the Wall, the landscape spreads out before you in a breathtaking panorama. The Wall itself stretches out endlessly to the horizon in both directions, a monumental barrier against the chaos beyond. The Wasteland on the other side is a desolate expanse, marked by barren land and scattered ruins. The wind is strong up here, filling your ears and making normal conversation difficult. Nestled in a sheltered nook is a makeshift camp, complete with a lookout post and a small, flickering campfire.

From the shadows, a lean figure emerges. He's a wiry man with sandy blond hair and sharp green eyes that seem to take in every detail. He's dressed in dark green studded leather armor, blending seamlessly with his surroundings. The man regards you with a mischievous grin, his eyes twinkling with a mix of curiosity and amusement. "Welcome to my perch," he says, his voice carrying a hint of humor. "What brings you to this forsaken height?"

Activities

Consult with Skywatcher Finn: Engage with Finn to gather information about the terrain and potential threats beyond the Wall.

Scout the Wasteland: Use the vantage point to observe and plan the next steps of your journey, identifying key locations and hazards.

Defend Against Attacks: After descending the Wall, prepare for possible attacks from Guardian Sentinels and a band of Scavengers drawn to the activity at the Wall's base.

Consult with Skywatcher Finn

Engage with Finn to gather information about the terrain and potential threats beyond the Wall. Finn's knowledge can

provide crucial insights for planning your next steps.

Terrain Overview

Finn provides a detailed description of the immediate landscape beyond the Wall, highlighting key features such as the mutated forest and the distant urban ruins that still bear signs of activity. Although his vantage point is a mile high, Finn possesses a spyglass which allows him to observe details beyond the Wall that no one else has witnessed.

He points out safe pathways and dangerous zones, emphasizing areas where mutated creatures have been spotted.

Potential Threats

Guardian Sentinels: Finn warns about the large metal constructs that patrol the area near the base of the Wall. He describes their capabilities and offers strategies for avoiding or defeating them.

Scavenger Gangs: Finn shares intel about the bands of Scavengers that roam the area. He explains their tactics, known territories, and how best to avoid confrontations with them.

Resources and Points of Interest

Water Source: Finn indicates the direction of the old water source that once supported the Lifeline Pipeline, explaining the potential challenges in accessing it.

The Lifeline Pipeline: He describes the Lifeline Pipeline, its purpose, and its historical connection to the original water source. Finn stresses the need to restore the pipeline to bring water back to Utopia.

Personal Guidance

Scout's Perspective: Finn offers to join the party on their journey, providing his expertise as a scout. His presence grants the party advantage on Survival checks to navigate the Wasteland.

Unique Insights: Finn shares personal anecdotes and historical knowledge about the Wall and the world beyond, adding depth to the PCs' understanding of their environment.

Example Dialogue

Finn looks out over the vast expanse beyond the Wall, his sharp eyes scanning the horizon. "Out there," he begins, pointing to the thick canopy below, "is the mutated forest, a place where nature's gone haywire. The trees themselves seem to want to tear you apart, and the creatures... well, let's just say they're not friendly." He shifts his gaze to the distant city ruins. "That city is where you'll find most of the trouble. Scavenger gangs rule the streets, and the guardian constructs patrol the old-world structures. Avoid their territories if you can or be ready for a fight."

He turns back to you, his expression serious. "You'll need to find the old water source to find out why the pipeline stopped flowing. The Lifeline Pipeline runs from there back through the Wall. Restoring that pipeline is your best shot at bringing water back to Utopia. But beware, the path is fraught with danger, and the water won't flow without power and working pumps. If the issue is an exhausted reservoir, you'll have to search for a new clean water source. But if the problem lies with the pipeline itself, you can probably find the necessary parts to repair it in the city ruins." Finn pauses, then grins. "I can guide you, if you'll have me. I've seen enough through my spyglass to know a thing or two about surviving out there."

DC Checks for Engaging with Finn

Persuasion Check: PCs must make a DC 15 Charisma (Persuasion) check to convince Finn to share his detailed knowledge and potentially join their party. If they appeal to his sense of duty or curiosity, they gain advantage on the roll.

Insight Check: A successful DC 15 Wisdom (Insight) check allows PCs to gauge Finn's true intentions and determine the sincerity of his offer to help.

Benefits of Consulting Finn

Terrain Knowledge: Finn's guidance provides the party with advantage on Survival checks for navigating the Wasteland.

Strategic Planning: Finn's insights into potential threats and safe routes help the party avoid unnecessary encounters, granting advantage on Stealth checks to bypass enemies.

Historical Context: Finn's stories and knowledge of the Wall and beyond add rich lore to the campaign, enhancing the players' understanding and immersion in the world.

Scout the Wasteland

Use the vantage point to observe and plan the next steps of your journey, identifying key locations and hazards.

Observational Checks

Perception Check: Using Finn's spyglass, PCs can make a DC 15 Wisdom (Perception) check to identify key features in the landscape. Success reveals detailed information about the terrain, hazards, and points of interest.

Survival Check: A successful DC 15 Wisdom (Survival) check helps PCs identify safe pathways and potential dangers, such as areas prone to ambushes or natural hazards.

Identifying Key Locations

Mutated Forest (The Dumps): PCs can spot the dense, overgrown forest filled with bizarre, mutated flora and fauna. They notice unusual movement patterns, suggesting the presence of dangerous creatures.

Ruined City (Lost Angeles): The sprawling urban ruin partially reclaimed by nature is visible in the distance. PCs can see the crumbling buildings and identify potential entry points and areas likely controlled by Scavenger gangs.

Hidden Village (Hope Falls): With a high Perception check (DC 20), players might catch glimpses of a well-hidden village in the distance.

Hazard Identification

Guardian Sentinels: From their vantage point using Finn's spyglass, PCs can spot the large constructs patrolling certain areas, identifiable by their rhythmic movements and occasional bursts of light from their weapons.

Scavenger Gangs: PCs may observe small groups moving through the ruins of the ancient city, their aggressive posture and occasional skirmishes indicating their territorial nature.

Planning Next Steps

Route Selection: Based on their observations, PCs can plan the safest and most efficient routes to their next destinations. They can choose to avoid certain areas or prepare for inevitable encounters.

Resource Allocation: Identifying potential threats and points of interest allows PCs to better allocate their resources, ensuring they are prepared for the challenges ahead.

Base of the Wall

After the party descends the Wall, the DM has two options for potential combat encounters: an immediate ambush as the party reaches the base, or a more strategic encounter where the party sets up camp and prepares defenses before being attacked.

Option 1: Immediate Ambush

As the party descends the final stretch of the Wall, they become vulnerable to detection by the denizens of the Wasteland. The movement of multiple figures against the vast backdrop of the Wall can draw unwanted attention.

Perception Checks:

- Have PCs each make a DC 15 Wisdom (Perception) check as they near the base of the Wall.

- Success means they spot potential ambushers preparing to strike.

- Failure means they remain unaware of the impending danger.

Surprise Round:

Any PCs who fail their Perception check are caught off guard as they reach the base of the Wall, and the ambushers (a mix of Scavengers and/or Guardian Sentinels) get a surprise round. During this round:

- Ambushers can take one action each.

- PCs who failed their Perception checks are surprised and can't take actions or reactions.

Alternatively, the DM can rule that if at least one PC succeeds, there is enough time to warn the rest of the party before the ambushers strike. If all fail, proceed to the surprise round.Option 2: Camp Setup and Defense

Upon reaching the base of the Wall, the party realizes the need for rest and decides to set up camp in a relatively sheltered area nearby. This gives them time to prepare defenses but also allows potential enemies to gather and plan an attack.

Camp Setup:

- The PCs find a suitable location within 100-200 feet of the Wall's base.

- They have about an hour to set up camp and prepare defenses before nightfall.

Preparing Defenses:

- **Fortify Position**: PCs can use nearby debris, remnants of old structures, or natural features to create defensive positions.

  - DC 15 Intelligence or Wisdom (Survival) check to effectively use the environment.

  - Success grants a +2 bonus to AC when taking cover during combat.

- **Set Traps**: PCs can use their equipment and scavenged materials to create simple traps around the perimeter.

  - DC 15 Intelligence check using thieves' tools to set effective traps.

  - Successful traps deal 1d6 damage and may restrain or slow enemies (DC 13 Dexterity save to avoid).

- **Establish Watch**: PCs should establish a watch rotation for the night.

  - Each watch period requires a DC 15 Wisdom (Perception) check.

  - Success on these checks allows early warning of approaching enemies.

Defend Against Attacks

Guardian Sentinels Attack:

- The Guardian Sentinels patrol the Wall and are alerted to the PCs' presence by their activity. These sentinels are formidable opponents, with high AC and powerful attacks.

- **Tactical Advantage:** The party can use the terrain to their advantage. By taking cover and using higher ground, they can gain a +2 bonus to AC against ranged attacks.
- **Focus Fire:** Targeting the same Sentinel can help bring them down faster, reducing their overwhelming firepower.

Scavenger Ambush:

- A band of Scavengers, drawn by the commotion, decides to attack, hoping to loot valuable items from the players.
- **Pack Tactics:** Scavengers use pack tactics to overwhelm their opponents. PCs should try to break their formation to reduce their effectiveness.
- **Intimidation and Persuasion:** PCs can use a DC 15 Charisma (Intimidation or Persuasion) check to potentially dissuade the Scavengers from attacking or to create a temporary truce.

Managing Resources:

- **Healing and Buffs:** Ensure that players use their healing spells and buffs effectively. A well-timed healing spell or defensive buff can turn the tide of battle.
- **Rationing Supplies:** Players should be mindful of their resources. Using too many supplies in one encounter could leave them vulnerable in future battles.

Terrain

High Altitude: The perch is exposed to strong winds and sudden gusts, requiring PCs to make either a Strength (Athletics) check to hold their position, or a Dexterity (Acrobatics) check to maintain their balance (DC 12 for both). Failure on either check may cause a PC to fall prone or be pushed 5 feet in the direction of the wind.

Cramped Space: The area around the lookout post is narrow and cluttered, providing limited movement and making it difficult to engage in combat without falling or bumping into obstacles.

Lair Actions

On initiative count 20 (losing initiative ties), the Guardian's Perch invokes one of the following lair actions:

Sudden Gust: At the start of the round, a strong gust of wind sweeps across the perch. Each creature must make a DC 13 Strength saving throw or be pushed 10 feet and knocked prone.

Electromagnetic Pulse: Ancient technology embedded in the Wall activates, releasing an electromagnetic pulse. Each creature within 30 feet must make a DC 14 Constitution saving throw. On a failure, they take 2d6 lightning damage and any electronic or magical items they carry are disabled until the end of their next turn. On a success, they take half damage and their items are unaffected.

Blinding Light: The sun reflects off a metal surface, creating a blinding flash of light. Each creature must make a DC 12 Constitution saving throw or be blinded until the start of its next turn.

Scaling the Encounter

Beginning Players (PC levels 1-5)

- Reduce the number of hostile creatures and lower their stats.
- Decrease DCs for skill checks by 3-5 points.
- Simplify environmental hazards.

Intermediate Players (PC levels 6-10)

- Use standard encounter setups as described.
- Maintain original DCs for skill checks.
- Standard environmental hazards.

Advanced Players (PC levels 11+)

- Increase the number of hostile creatures and their stats.
- Raise DCs for skill checks by 2-4 points.
- Increase the complexity and intensity of environmental hazards.

Monsters

Guardian Sentinel

Scavenger (4-5)

NPC

Skywatcher Finn: A reclusive scout with valuable insight about the terrain and dangers beyond the Wall.

Act 3

Act 3 – Beyond the Wall

The Dumps

The mutated forest, known by locals as the Dumps, is a hazardous area filled with mutated flora and fauna. Players must navigate through these dense, eerie woods to reach the city ruins of Lost Angeles or the secluded village of Hope Falls, facing environmental challenges and hostile creatures along the way. Key encounters include mutated wildlife, toxic plants, and natural hazards. Despite the contrast with the desert of the Wasteland, all liquid in the Dumps, such as any pools of water or streams, is poisonous. The Dumps is a failed biochemical experiment to create artificial water.

As you enter the dense, overgrown forest, a sense of foreboding washes over you. The air is thick with humidity, and the canopy above blocks out most of the sunlight, casting eerie shadows on the forest floor. Strange, twisted trees loom overhead, their branches intertwined like skeletal fingers reaching for the sky. The ground is uneven and covered in a carpet of thick, spongy moss that squelches underfoot. Every step is accompanied by the rustling of unseen creatures and the distant, haunting calls of mutated wildlife.

The atmosphere is heavy with the sickly-sweet odor of decaying vegetation and the faint, acrid scent of toxic plants. Vibrant, bioluminescent fungi cling to the tree trunks, casting an otherworldly glow that illuminates the path ahead. As you push deeper into the forest, the oppressive silence is occasionally broken by the sounds of dripping water and the distant rumble of something large moving through the underbrush. However, any pools of water or streams you encounter emit a faint, unnatural glow, and a closer inspection reveals the liquid to be thick and viscous, giving off a noxious smell. This place, though rich in vegetation, hides deadly secrets within its seemingly lush surroundings.

Activities

Navigate the Forest: Players must use (Wisdom) Survival checks to find safe paths through the forest and avoid natural hazards like quicksand and poisonous fungi patches.

Confront Environmental Hazards: Engage in combat with mutated organisms such as Fungal Hulks and Mutant Vines.

Protect the Lifeline Pipeline: Defend the pipeline from attacks by Toxic Sludge.

Find a Path Through the Dumps

To navigate through the Dumps, PCs must utilize their skills in Survival and Perception to find a safe path amidst the hazardous environment. The forest is a tangled maze of mutated vegetation, and the presence of toxic liquids and aggressive wildlife adds to the challenge. Here's how the party can successfully find their way:

Skill Checks and Guidance

Using Skills:

- **Survival Check:** PCs can make a DC 15 Wisdom (Survival) check to identify a safe route through the forest. Success indicates they have found a path that avoids major hazards like quicksand and venomous vines. Failure results in encountering additional hazards or taking longer to navigate. Survival checks can also be used to reveal helpful information or natural indicators such as tracks, markers, changes in vegetation, or other wilderness signs which may suggest safer (or more dangerous) paths.

- **Perception Check:** PCs can make a DC 15 Wisdom (Perception) check to spot immediate dangers such as lurking creatures or hidden traps. Success allows them to avoid these dangers, while failure may trigger an encounter or trap.

Guidance from NPCs: If the PCs have Pipemaster Jax in their party, they gain advantage on all checks related to navigating a path through the Dumps. Jax's knowledge of the pipelines and the surrounding areas can provide valuable insights and shortcuts.

Detailed Steps for Navigating

Initial Navigation: At the start, each PC may make a DC 15 Wisdom (Survival) check to determine the overall route they will take through the Dumps. Success means they have identified a viable path, while failure indicates they are likely to encounter more hazards.

Spotting Hazards: As they travel, PCs make frequent DC 15 Wisdom (Perception) checks to spot immediate hazards such as quicksand or venomous vines. Success allows them to avoid or prepare for these dangers, while failure may result in stepping into a hazard or triggering a trap.

Interpreting Clues: PCs can search for markers left by local travelers or natural indicators of safety. A DC 15 Wisdom (Survival) check can reveal helpful information, guiding them through the forest. Success provides clear directions, while failure may lead to confusion or backtracking.

Using Environmental Puzzles: Certain areas may require solving environmental puzzles to proceed. For example, PCs might need to align certain symbols or activate ancient mechanisms to clear a path. These puzzles require a combination of Intelligence (Arcana) and Dexterity (Sleight of Hand) checks, typically at DC 15.

Environmental Encounters in the Dumps

Fungal Grove: A dense cluster of bioluminescent fungi creating an eerie glow.

Quicksand Mire: A large area of quicksand hidden beneath a thin layer of leaves and debris.

The Lifeline Pipeline: A section of the ancient pipeline that continues from the Wall running through the forest, under attack by Toxic Sludges.

Fungal Grove

A dense cluster of bioluminescent fungi creating an eerie glow. The fungi emit a soft, pulsating light that bathes the grove in an otherworldly luminescence. The air is thick with the sweet, sickly smell of decay, and the ground is spongy underfoot, covered in a carpet of fungal growth. The bioluminescent fungi range in size from small mushrooms to towering fungal trees, their caps glowing in shades of blue, green, and purple.

Encounter: As PCs make their way through the fungal grove, they encounter several Fungal Hulks. These hulking creatures, covered in glowing fungi, are slow but incredibly strong. They release toxic spores into the air, creating a dangerous environment for the party.

Activity: To safely traverse the grove without disturbing the spores, players must solve a puzzle. The puzzle involves navigating a safe path through the fungi by identifying non-toxic fungi clusters. This requires keen observation and understanding of the environment.

Puzzle

Setup: The grove is divided into a 5x5 grid, with each square containing a different type of fungi. Players must determine which squares are safe to pass through by identifying the non-toxic fungi. The toxic fungi are characterized by their brighter glow and the presence of small, pulsing nodules on their stems. You can use the following table for your 5x5 grid or create your own.

Glowcap (Non-Toxic)	Luminshroom (Non-Toxic)	Faelight Mushroom (Non-Toxic)	Glowcap (Non-Toxic)	Luminshroom (Non-Toxic)
Faelight Mushroom (Non-Toxic)	Sporeburst Fungus (Highly Toxic)	Necrofungus (Highly Toxic)	Glowcap (Non-Toxic)	Luminshroom (Non-Toxic)
Glowcap (Non-Toxic)	HallucinoShroom (Highly Toxic)	Faelight Mushroom (Non-Toxic)	Nightshade Fungus (Non-Toxic)	Glowcap (Non-Toxic)
Radiant Puffball (Non-Toxic)	Faelight Mushroom (Non-Toxic)	Venomthorn Fungus (Highly Toxic)	Dreamspore Fungus (Moderately Toxic)	Glowcap (Non-Toxic)
Glowcap (Non-Toxic)	Nightshade Fungus (Non-Toxic)	Radiant Puffball (Non-Toxic)	Faelight Mushroom (Non-Toxic)	Luminshroom (Non-Toxic)

Observation: PCs must make a DC 15 Wisdom (Nature or Survival) check to notice the subtle differences between the toxic and non-toxic fungi. On a success, they can identify the squares that are safe to enter. Each PC can make only one skill check per turn.

- **Memory:** Once a PC identifies a safe square, they must remember it and communicate it to the group. PCs can make a DC 12 Intelligence (Investigation) check to recall the pattern of safe squares if they get confused.

- **Sequence:** PCs must step on the safe squares while crossing the grove to avoid disturbing the hazardous spores. Stepping on a toxic square releases a cloud of spores, forcing all creatures within a 10-foot radius to make a DC 15 Constitution saving throw or be poisoned for 1 hour.

- **Teamwork:** PCs can work together, using their combined knowledge and skills to navigate the puzzle. They can make DC 15 Intelligence (Nature) checks to deduce which fungi are safe based on their collective observations.

Penalties for Failure:

- If PCs step on a toxic square, they must deal with the effects of the spores and potentially attract the attention of nearby Fungal Hulks.

- Each failed check or misstep increases the likelihood of encountering additional Fungal Hulks, as any disturbance in the grove draws them closer.

Rewards for Success:

- Successfully navigating the puzzle without disturbing the spores allows the party to pass through the grove unharmed.

- PCs who solve the puzzle can find valuable resources in the form of rare fungi with medicinal properties. These can be used to create antidotes or healing potions, providing a significant advantage for the journey ahead.

Fungal Table

Below is a table of information on various fungi found in the fungal grove:

Name	Description	Properties	Type	Category	Toxicity Level and Effect
Glowcap	Small mushrooms with bright blue caps that emit a soft, pulsating light	Provides dim light in a 10-foot radius	Non-Toxic	Bioluminescent	Non-Toxic; Safe to touch and walk on
Luminshroom	Tall mushrooms with bioluminescent caps that glow in shades of green and purple	Can be used to create a potion of darkvision	Non-Toxic	Bioluminescent	Non-Toxic; Safe to touch and walk on
Radiant Puffball	Round fungi with a faint, steady glow and small pulsing nodules on their stems	Emits a faint, steady light	Non-Toxic	Bioluminescent	Non-Toxic; Safe to touch and walk on
Sporeburst Fungus	Large, bulbous fungi with bright red caps covered in small nodules	Releases a burst of spores when disturbed, causes 1d6 poison dmg on contact	Toxic	Spore-Emitting	Highly Toxic; Causes 1d6 poison dmg on contact, DC 15 Con save vs poisoned condition
HallucinoShroom	Mushrooms with multicolored caps that shimmer and change color	Causes vivid hallucinations if inhaled	Toxic	Hallucinogenic	Highly Toxic; Causes vivid hallucinations, DC 15 Constitution save vs poisoned condition
Necrofungus	Dark, twisted fungi with black caps and a faint, sickly-sweet odor	Drains 1d4 hit points on contact	Toxic	Necrotic	Highly Toxic; Drains 1d4 hit points on contact, DC 15 Con save vs poisoned condition
Venomthorn Fungus	Green, thorn-covered fungi that exude a sticky, toxic sap	Causes 1d6 poison damage on contact	Toxic	Poisonous	Highly Toxic; Causes 1d6 poison dmg on contact, DC 15 Con save vs poisoned condition
Nightshade Fungus	Black fungi with deep purple streaks and a faint glow	Can be used to create a poison or antidote	Non-Toxic	Bioluminescent	Non-Toxic; Can be harvested for crafting purposes
Faelight Mushroom	Pale blue mushrooms with a steady, soft glow	Provides dim light in a 5-foot radius	Non-Toxic	Bioluminescent	Non-Toxic; Safe to touch and walk on
Dreamspore Fungus	Large fungi with soft pink caps and a sweet fragrance	Causes drowsiness if inhaled	Toxic	Hallucinogenic	Moderately Toxic; Causes drowsiness, DC 12 Con save vs poisoned condition for 1d4 hours

Quicksand Mire

A large area of quicksand lies hidden beneath a thin layer of leaves and debris. The ground looks deceptively solid, but any misstep could lead to a dangerous entrapment. The air here is thick with humidity, and the occasional bubbling of the quicksand can be heard, adding to the eerie atmosphere.

Encounter: PCs must navigate this treacherous terrain with caution. As they progress, they may encounter areas where the ground suddenly gives way, pulling them into the mire. The quicksand is difficult to escape once ensnared, and struggling only makes it worse.

Avoiding the Quicksand

Check: PCs must make a DC 15 Wisdom (Survival) check to spot the signs of quicksand hidden beneath the foliage.

Failure: On a failed check, the PC steps into quicksand and must immediately make a DC 15 Strength saving throw to avoid being trapped. If they fail this check, they become restrained and start sinking.

Escaping the Quicksand

Check: Creatures who are trapped in the quicksand must make a DC 15 Strength (Athletics) check to free themselves. They can attempt this check once per turn.

Assistance: Other players can assist, providing advantage on the check, but they must make a DC 12 Dexterity (Athletics or Acrobatics) check to avoid being trapped themselves while helping.

Progression: Each failed escape attempt causes the trapped creature to sink deeper, increasing the DC by 1 for each subsequent check. If a creature fails three times, they are fully submerged and require immediate rescue.

Finding a Safe Path

Check: PCs can make a DC 15 Wisdom (Survival) check to identify a safe path around the mire.

Success: On a successful check, the PC marks a clear path for the party to follow, avoiding the quicksand entirely.

Failure: On a failed check, the PCs misidentify the terrain, leading the party into another area of quicksand, requiring another sequence of Survival and Athletics checks to avoid or escape it.

The Lifeline Pipeline

A section of the ancient pipeline, known as the Lifeline Pipeline, continues from the Wall, running through the dense and treacherous forest. This crucial segment is currently under attack by Toxic Sludges, threatening the vital water supply needed for the mission. The pipeline is rusted and corroded in many places, making it prone to leaks and structural failures.

Encounter: PCs must defend the pipeline from the aggressive Toxic Sludges while simultaneously making necessary repairs to ensure the water flow remains uninterrupted. The environment is hostile, with the dense foliage providing limited visibility and maneuverability.

Identifying Damages

Check: PCs must make a DC 15 Intelligence (Investigation) or Wisdom (Perception) check to identify the damaged sections of the pipeline.

Success: On a successful check, the player identifies a critical pipe rupture or break that needs immediate attention.

Failure: On a failed check, the player misidentifies the issue, leading to wasted time and potential escalation of the sludge attack.

Repairing the Pipeline

Check: PCs must use a DC 15 Intelligence (Technology) check or Dexterity check using engineer's tools to repair the damaged sections.

Success: On a successful check, the PC repairs a section of the pipeline, restoring partial functionality.

Failure: On a failed check, the repair attempt fails, and the character must try again on their next turn, increasing the pressure as more Toxic Sludges arrive.

Assistance: Other characters can assist in the repair process, providing advantage on the check, but they risk being attacked by sludge while doing so.

Defending Against Toxic Sludge

Combat: PCs must fend off waves of Toxic Sludge creatures that are attacking the pipeline.

Tactics: The sludges target characters closest to the pipeline, such as those actively working on repairs. PCs must coordinate their defense and repair actions to succeed.

Reinforcements: If the battle extends, more Toxic Sludges may join the fray, increasing the difficulty.

Terrain and Environmental Hazards

The terrain in the Dumps is treacherous and unpredictable. The forest floor is covered with thick, uneven vegetation, creating difficult terrain. PCs attempting to move at normal speed must make frequent DC 15 Dexterity (Athletics or Acrobatics) checks to avoid tripping or getting entangled in the undergrowth. Natural hazards like quicksand and venomous vines require DC 15 Wisdom (Survival or Nature) checks to identify and Strength (Athletics) or Dexterity (Acrobatics) checks to navigate safely. The bioluminescent fungi provide dim light, but areas of darkness can still pose a challenge for those without darkvision.

Hazards from Liquid in the Dumps

The players should be cautious regarding liquids in the Dumps. Any pools of water or streams they encounter are irreparably poisoned, a result of a failed biochemical experiment. It is essential for PCs to test or purify any water they consider drinking or using. Any items or equipment that come into contact with the poisonous liquid must be carefully, thoroughly cleaned, or they may transfer the poison to the player handling them.

Contact with Liquid: If a character comes into contact with any liquid from the Dumps, they must make a DC 15 Constitution saving throw or be poisoned for 1 hour. While poisoned in this way, the character suffers from hallucinations and disadvantage on all attack rolls and ability checks.

Ingestion of Liquid: If a character accidentally drinks the liquid, they must make a DC 20 Constitution saving throw. On a failed save, the character takes 2d6 poison damage and is poisoned for 24 hours, during which they suffer from severe hallucinations, disadvantage on all attack rolls and ability checks. On a successful save, the player takes half damage and is poisoned for only 1 hour.

Other Environmental Hazards

Bioluminescent Fungi: These fungi provide dim light within a 20-foot radius but can also cause distraction. PCs must make a DC 10 Wisdom saving throw to avoid being momentarily blinded by a sudden change in light,

which imposes disadvantage on the next action they take.

Quicksand: Quicksand pits are hidden throughout the forest. Characters who step into quicksand must make a DC 15 Strength (Athletics) check to free themselves. Failure results in being restrained, and further checks must be made to escape.

Lair Actions

On initiative count 20 (losing initiative ties), the Dumps invokes one of the following lair actions:

Toxic Spore Release: A burst of toxic spores fills a 20-foot radius area. Each creature in that area must make a DC 15 Constitution saving throw or be poisoned for 1 minute. While poisoned, the creature is also blinded.

Vine Entanglement: Hostile Mutant Vines erupt from the ground in a 20-foot radius area. Each creature within that area must succeed on a DC 15 Strength saving throw or be restrained. A restrained creature can use its action to make a DC 15 Strength check, freeing itself on a success. The vines wither away after 1 minute.

Maddening Hallucinations: A psychic pulse pervades the area, causing creatures within a 30-foot radius to experience vivid hallucinations. Each creature must make a DC 15 Wisdom saving throw or be confused (as per the *Confusion* spell) for 1 minute.

Scaling The Encounter

Beginning Players (PC levels 1-5)

General Adjustments

- Reduce the number of hostile creatures in each encounter.
- Lower DCs for skill checks by 3-5 points.
- Decrease the frequency and intensity of environmental hazards.

Fungal Hulks

- Reduce the number of Fungal Hulks to 1-2 per encounter.
- Lower their AC to 13 and hit points to 40.

Toxic Sludge

- Reduce the number of Toxic Sludge creatures to 1-2 per encounter.
- Lower their AC to 14 and hit points to 35.

Environmental Hazards

- DCs for navigating the Dumps: 12
- DCs for avoiding quicksand: 10
- DCs for avoiding poisoning from liquids: 10

Lair Actions

- **Toxic Spore Release**: DC 12 Constitution saving throw
- **Vine Entanglement**: DC 12 Strength saving throw
- **Maddening Hallucinations**: DC 12 Wisdom saving throw

Intermediate Players (PC levels 6-10)

General Adjustments

- Use standard encounter setups as described.
- Maintain original DCs for skill checks.
- Standard frequency and intensity of environmental hazards.

Fungal Hulks: Use standard number and stats.

Toxic Sludge: Use standard number and stats.

Environmental Hazards

- DCs for navigating the Dumps: 15
- DCs for avoiding quicksand: 15
- DCs for avoiding poisoning from liquids: 15

Lair Actions

- **Toxic Spore Release**: DC 15 Constitution saving throw
- **Vine Entanglement**: DC 15 Strength saving throw
- **Maddening Hallucinations**: DC 15 Wisdom saving throw

Advanced Players (PC levels 11+)

General Adjustments

- Increase the number of hostile creatures in each encounter.
- Raise DCs for skill checks by 2-4 points.
- Increase the frequency and intensity of environmental hazards.

Fungal Hulks

- Increase the number of Fungal Hulks to 3-4 per encounter.
- Increase AC to 16 and hit points to 80.

Toxic Sludge

- Increase the number of Toxic Sludge creatures to 3-4 per encounter.

- Increase AC to 17 and hit points to 70.

Environmental Hazards

- DCs for navigating the Dumps: 17
- DCs for avoiding quicksand: 17
- DCs for avoiding poisoning from liquids: 17

Lair Actions

- **Toxic Spore Release**: DC 17 Constitution saving throw
- **Vine Entanglement**: DC 17 Strength saving throw
- **Maddening Hallucinations**: DC 17 Wisdom saving throw

Monsters

Fungal Hulk (2-3)

Toxic Sludge (2-3)

Mutant Vine

Lost Angeles

Players must navigate the urban ruins of Lost Angeles, seeking parts to repair piping or old pumps to restore functionality to the pipes. They encounter environmental hazards, mutated creatures, and the local Scavenger faction led by Kael.

Guide PCs through the city to find a pump and necessary parts, deal with various dangers and negotiate with or combat Scavengers.

Before you stretch the vast remnants of a ruined city. As you enter its borders, crumbling skyscrapers loom overhead, their jagged silhouettes jutting against the sky as nature slowly reclaims the ruins. Everywhere are shattered windows and cracked walls as far as the eye can see, while the occasional flicker of old-world technology sparks to life in the shadows. The fractured pavement is littered with debris, from broken glass to rusted metal, making each step a cautious endeavor.

The breeze carries with it the scent of decay, and you can almost feel the faint hum of residual energy. As you move deeper into the heart of the city, the sounds of distant scurrying and the creaking of unstable structures echo around you. Pools of stagnant water, glowing faintly with an unnatural light, dot the landscape, and the occasional glimpse of movement hints at unseen dangers lurking just out of sight. Despite the city's desolation, a sense of foreboding and the promise of valuable resources draw you further into the ruins.

Activities

Find Parts, Repair and Relocate the Pump: Locate a pump and gather the necessary parts to fix it.

Explore Key Locations: Explore the Pump Station, the Tech Lab and the Market Square.

Investigate Ruined Buildings: This is a city filled with buildings that the PCs may want to explore.

The Pump Station

An old facility with a large, rusted pump that once transported water throughout the city. The Pump Station is a critical location for restoring water flow to the Lifeline Pipeline, but the years have not been kind to it. The machinery is covered in rust and a thick layer of grime, indicating years of disuse. PCs must navigate the station, gather necessary parts, and repair the pump while defending against lurking threats.

Find Parts, Repair and Relocate the Pump

PCs must locate the old water pump within the dilapidated Pump Station and gather the necessary parts to restore its functionality. After repairing the pump, they must figure out how to move it to the Lifeline Pipeline. This involves navigating through dangerous terrain, dealing with aggressive creatures, and solving logistical challenges. The pump, once a crucial component of the city's water system, is now a rusted relic of the past, surrounded by debris and overgrown with vegetation.

Locate the Pump

Check: PCs must make a DC 15 Intelligence (Investigation) check to locate the pump within the cluttered and darkened Pump Station. Success reveals the pump's location, partially buried under debris.

Success: PCs find the pump, noting its condition and the parts needed for repair.

Failure: PCs waste valuable time searching and may encounter hostile creatures attracted by the noise.

DM Note: When describing how the party finds the pump and its condition, keep in mind that the old water pump is a rather large piece of machinery, standing at 8 feet tall and 6 feet wide.

Assess the Damage

Check: PCs must make a DC 15 Intelligence (Technology) check to assess the pump's condition and identify the missing or damaged parts.

Success: PCs successfully identify the required parts and the extent of the damage.

Failure: PCs misjudge the damage, leading to potential complications during the repair process.

Gather Necessary Parts

Location: The Tech Lab

- **Description:** The lab houses old-world technology, including crucial pump parts.
- **Activity:** Locate and retrieve the necessary components for the pump.
- **Encounter:** Old-world security drones still patrol the lab.

Location: The Market Square

- **Description:** An open area where Scavengers trade goods and information, now overrun by mutant wildlife.
- **Activity:** Search for and acquire additional pump parts from Scavenger caches.
- **Encounter:** Defend against attacks from aggressive mutant creatures.

Repair the Pump

Check: Once all the necessary parts have been gathered, one PC must use a DC 15 Intelligence (Technology) check or a Dexterity check using engineer's tools to repair the damaged sections of the pump.

Success: On a successful check, the PC repairs a section of the pump, restoring partial functionality.

Failure: On a failed check, the repair attempt fails, and the PC must try again on their next turn, increasing the pressure as more Sun Blights arrive.

Assistance: Other PCs can assist in the repair process, providing advantage on the check, but they risk being attacked by the Sun Blights while assisting.

Relocate the Pump

The pump, a massive and cumbersome piece of machinery, stands at about 8 feet tall and 6 feet wide, weighing approximately 1,500 pounds. It is designed to be stationary and was not meant to be moved easily. The task ahead involves relocating this pump from its current position in Lost Angeles to the Water Source Facility at Hope Falls, a journey spanning several miles through the treacherous terrain of the Dumps and beyond. The party must devise a strategy to transport the pump while fending off attacks and navigating environmental hazards along the way.

Assess the Pump's Weight and Size

- **Check:** PCs must evaluate the pump's dimensions and weight to understand the logistics of moving it. This requires a DC 15 Intelligence (Technology or Investigation) check.

- **Success:** PCs accurately assess the pump's size and weight, allowing them to plan the transportation effectively.

- **Failure:** PCs underestimate the difficulty, leading to complications in their transportation plan.

Construct a Transportation Device

- **Check:** PCs must use a DC 15 Intelligence check using engineer's tools or a Dexterity check using carpenter's tools to build a makeshift transport device, such as a sled or wheeled platform, to move the pump.

- **Success:** PCs successfully construct a device capable of transporting the pump.

- **Failure:** The device is unstable or ineffective, requiring further attempts or leading to delays.

Move the Pump

- **Check:** PCs must make a series of DC 15 Strength (Athletics) checks to move the pump out of the Pump Station and onto the transport device. This will require coordination and teamwork.

- **Success:** The pump is securely placed on the transport device.

- **Failure:** The pump slips or is dropped, causing delays and potential damage (1d6 damage to the pump per failed check).

Transport the Pump Across the Dumps

- **Check:** The party must navigate the pump through the dense forest of the Dumps, making DC 15 Strength (Athletics) checks to pull or push the transport device over uneven terrain. They must also make DC 15 Dexterity (Athletics or Technology) checks to avoid obstacles and hazards.

- **Encounters:** During this journey, the party will face attacks from Sun Blights and other creatures. They must defend the pump while ensuring it remains on the transport device.

- **Success:** The pump progresses steadily towards the Water Source Facility in Hope Falls.

- **Failure:** The pump may become stuck or damaged, requiring additional repairs and potentially attracting more creatures.

Defend the Pump

- **Encounter:** PCs must fend off waves of Sun Blights attacking the pump during the relocation process.

- **Reinforcements:** If the battle extends, more Sun Blights may join the fray, increasing the difficulty.

Overcome Environmental Challenges

- **Check:** PCs must make DC 15 Wisdom (Survival) checks to navigate around quicksand, toxic plants, and collapsing structures.

- **Success:** PCs successfully navigate the terrain, maintaining steady progress.

- **Failure:** PCs encounter additional hazards or delays, potentially damaging the pump or attracting more creatures.

Secure the Pump at Hope Falls

- **Final Check:** Upon reaching the water source in Hope Falls, PCs must make a final DC 15 Strength (Athletics) or Intelligence (Technology) check to secure the pump in its new location, ready to be connected to the Lifeline Pipeline.

- **Success:** The pump is successfully relocated and ready for operation.

- **Failure:** The pump requires final adjustments, delaying the connection process.

Sun Blight Encounter

Initial Trigger: This encounter can be triggered in two ways:

1. If the PCs fail their DC 15 Intelligence (Investigation) check to locate the pump, or

2. When the PCs return to repair the pump with their newly acquired parts

As the PCs search for or begin work on the pump, the vibrations and noise disturb a nest of Sun Blights that have made their home in the overgrown vegetation surrounding the pump. These aggressive, plant-like creatures are drawn to the activity, seeing the PCs as both intruders and potential nutrients.

Encounter Details

*   **Number of Sun Blights**: Initially 1d4+1, with 1d4 more arriving every 3 rounds of combat or failed repair check.

*   **Sun Blight Behavior**: The creatures attack in waves, attempting to overwhelm and entangle the PCs.

*   **Environmental Factors**: The cluttered pump station provides both cover and hazards. PCs can use debris for cover, but difficult terrain slows movement.

Combat Dynamics

*   The Sun Blights use hit-and-run tactics, striking quickly and retreating into the overgrowth.

*   They prioritize targets actively working on the pump.

*   Every failed repair check not only brings more Sun Blights but also risks damaging the pump further.

Resolution

*   The encounter continues until either all Sun Blights are defeated or driven off, or the pump is successfully repaired.

*   If the PCs retreat, they'll need to clear out the Sun Blights before they can safely work on the pump.

The Tech Lab

A partially collapsed building housing old-world technology, including crucial pump parts. Despite the damage, the lab's remnants of sophisticated equipment and consoles still flicker with static, hinting at the advanced technology that once thrived here. PCs must locate and retrieve the components needed to restore the pump, all while navigating hazards and deactivating security systems.

Below is a table of the necessary pump parts that can be found in the Tech Lab:

Tech Lab Components Table

Component Name	Description	Location	Specific DC Check to Find
Power Core	A compact, cylindrical device emitting a faint blue glow	Tech Lab's central power station	DC 15 Intelligence (Investigation)
Filtration Module	A rectangular, metal box with various pipes and filters attached	Storage room filled with various spare parts	DC 12 Wisdom (Perception)
Pressure Regulator	A brass-colored device with dials and gauges, partially rusted	Attached to an old, rusted pump mechanism	DC 14 Intelligence (Investigation)
Circuit Board	A green circuit board with intricate wiring and small blinking lights	Embedded within a control panel on the wall	DC 16 Wisdom (Perception)
Coolant System	A metal canister with cooling fins and a liquid coolant reservoir	Compartment near the back of the lab, protected by Advanced Security Drones	DC 18 Intelligence (Investigation); DC 15 Technology check to disable

Locate and Retrieve the Necessary Components

Searching the Lab

Check: PCs must search the lab for the pump parts. At the DM's discretion, this can be done as multiple checks for specific parts, new checks through searching multiple rooms, or a single skill check (either Investigation or Perception) from each PC. For the single check option, use the DCs from the table above to determine which parts are found. If any PC succeeds at a DC 18 on either type of check, all components are found.

Success: Players find all the needed components amidst the debris and old equipment.

Failure: Players fail to locate all the parts they expect to be able to find here and must continue searching, which risks triggering additional security measures.

Deactivating Security Systems

Check: PCs must disable the Advanced Security Drones and security systems to safely retrieve the parts, requiring either a DC 15 Intelligence (Technology) check using engineer's tools OR a DC 15 Dexterity (Technology) check using thieves' tools.

Success: PCs successfully deactivate the security systems and drones.

Failure: Advanced Security Drones activate and attack the party.

Combat Encounter: Advanced Security Drones

Encounter: Unless they are successfully disabled beforehand, several Advanced Security Drones detect the PCs' presence as they navigate the lab and engage the party in combat.

Combat: PCs must defend themselves against the drones while ensuring the safety of the retrieved components.

Extracting the Components

Check: Once the drones are dealt with, PCs must carefully extract some of the components, requiring a DC 15 Dexterity (Technology) check using engineer's tools or thieves' tools to safely remove equipment (such as the Circuit Board, Power Core and Pressure Regulator) without causing further damage.

Success: Components are safely extracted and ready for transport.

Failure: Mishandling causes damage to the parts, requiring additional checks or repairs.

The Market Square

The Market Square is a ruined trading hub where Scavengers trade goods and information under the watchful eye of Scavenger Leader Kael. PCs can attempt to gather intelligence and find additional pump parts while potentially negotiating with Kael, who demands a high price for any help. Each vendor in the Market Square has to pay protection money to Kael and his Scavengers.

Makeshift stalls and abandoned carts litter the area. As you step into the square, the oppressive silence is shattered by the low murmur of voices and the occasional clink of metal. Scavengers, drawn by the prospect of trade and survival, watch warily from the shadows, ready to either offer help or take advantage of the chaos. In the center of the square, you spot a crate marked with the symbol of the old world, hinting at the valuable contents within.

Half a dozen vendors, their faces marked by the harshness of survival, operate makeshift stalls, constantly under the watchful eyes of Kael's Scavengers.

Gather Intelligence:

Check: PCs must make a DC 14 Charisma (Persuasion) check to gather useful information from the Scavengers and vendors.

Success: The PCs learn the locations of key pump parts and potential hazards in the area.

Failure: The Scavengers and vendors are uncooperative, andPCs may have to resort to other means to gather information.

Find Additional Pump Parts:

Check: PCs can make a DC 15 Intelligence (Investigation) check to find the components hidden among the debris and abandoned stalls scattered throughout the Market Square.

Success: They locate a crate containing the necessary pump parts.

Failure: The search takes longer, potentially drawing more attention from Kael's Scavengers.

Market Vendors

Vendor 1: Ratchet

Ratchet was once an engineer in a small enclave, but after a raid led by Kael's Scavengers, he was forced to flee to Lost Angeles. With his technical skills, Ratchet salvages and repairs old-world technology, but Kael's gang demands a heavy price for his safety. Ratchet pays 40% of his earnings to Kael's gang as protection money, leaving him barely enough to survive.

Protection Money Paid: 40% of earnings

Table of Products Sold:

Name	Description	Properties	Price
Circuit Boards	Old-world circuit boards used for various repairs	Necessary for repairing advanced technology	20 gp
Servo Motors	Small motors used in robotics and automation	Grants advantage on mechanical repair checks	15 gp
Pump Components	Various parts needed to repair the pump	Necessary for pump repair (DC 15 Investigation check)	30 gp
Solar Panels	Small, portable solar panels for generating electricity	Can be used to power small devices	50 gp

Information:

Ratchet knows the exact location of the Water Source Facility, which lies in Hope Falls, and can provide directions to the hidden society.

He is aware of Kael's distrust of his lieutenants and believes that Kael's paranoia could be exploited to turn his followers against him.

Vendor 2: Stitch

Stitch was once a medic, known for her ability to patch up even the worst wounds. She set up shop in Lost Angeles to provide medical supplies and aid, but Kael's gang forces her to pay a hefty sum to continue her operations. Stitch pays a fixed fee of 30 gp per week for protection.

Protection Money Paid: 30 gp per week

Table of Products Sold:

Name	Description	Properties	Price
Healing Kits	Kits containing bandages, salves, and antiseptics	Heals 1d4+2 hit points per use	10 gp
Antitoxin	Vials of antitoxin for treating poison	Grants advantage on saving throws vs. poison	25 gp
Stimpacks	Injectors that provide a quick boost of energy	Restores 1d6 hit points and removes 1 level of exhaustion	15 gp
Surgical Tools	Tools for performing advanced medical procedures	Grants advantage on Medicine checks	30 gp

Information:

Stitch has heard rumors that the clean water source is heavily guarded by the hidden village in Hope Falls and that they use a water wheel to generate electricity.

She knows that Kael suffers from severe migraines and uses a specific herb for relief, which could be used to negotiate with or manipulate him.

Vendor 3: Scraps

Scraps is a young Scavenger who grew up in the ruins, learning to survive by salvaging anything of value. Kael's gang took him in, but only in exchange for a cut of his finds. Scraps pays 50% of his earnings as protection money, struggling to make ends meet.

Protection Money Paid: 50% of earnings

Table of Products Sold:

Name	Description	Properties	Price
Metal Scraps	Pieces of metal from various sources	Can be used to reinforce or repair structures	5 gp
Old Batteries	Batteries scavenged from old devices	Can power small devices for a limited time	10 gp
Tool Kits	Sets of basic tools for various purposes	Grants advantage on certain skill checks	20 gp
Gears and Springs	Small mechanical parts for crafting and repairs	Necessary for mechanical crafting and repairs	10 gp

Information:

Scraps knows the layout of Lost Angeles well and can guide the party to the location of the pump and other essential parts.

He has overheard that Kael's faction is planning a major raid soon, which could be used to either avoid confrontation or set a trap.

Vendor 4: Grit

Grit was once a farmer, but the harsh conditions of the Wasteland forced him to abandon his land. Now, he trades in Lost Angeles, dealing in seeds and preserved foods. Kael's gang takes a significant portion of his goods, making survival a constant struggle. Grit provides food supplies to Kael's gang in exchange for protection.

Protection Money Paid: Provides food supplies to Kael's gang

Table of Products Sold:

Name	Description	Properties	Price
Dried Rations	Preserved food that lasts for months	Provides sustenance for one day	1 gp
Seeds	Seeds for growing various crops	Can be used to start small gardens	2 gp
Water Purifiers	Devices for purifying small amounts of water	Removes impurities and toxins from water	15 gp
Herbal Remedies	Natural remedies for minor ailments	Grants advantage on saving throws vs. disease	10 gp

Information:

Grit knows about a hidden path to Hope Falls, where the water source is located, that avoids most of the dangers of the Wasteland.

He has information on Kael's food storage locations, which could be useful for sabotaging his supplies or negotiating with him.

Vendor 5: Clank

Clank is an ex-mechanic who turned to trading machinery parts after losing his workshop to a Scavenger raid. Kael's gang keeps a tight leash on him, demanding a large share of his profits. Clank's knowledge of old-world machinery is invaluable, but the protection fees are crippling. Clank pays Kael's gang by providing repair services for their equipment.

Protection Money Paid: Provides repair services for Kael's equipment

Table of Products Sold:

Name	Description	Properties	Price
Engine Parts	Components for repairing engines	Necessary for vehicle repairs	25 gp
Hydraulic Fluid	Fluid used in various machinery	Essential for maintaining machinery	5 gp
Welding Kits	Kits for welding and repairing metal	Grants advantage on crafting and repair checks	15 gp
Mechanical Manuals	Manuals with instructions for various repairs	Grants advantage on Intelligence (Technology) checks (may be limited to certain categories at DM's discretion)	50 gp

Information:

Clank has heard that the water storage building in Hope Falls is critical for the region's water supply and that it's heavily fortified.

He knows that Kael's gang has several hidden caches of old-world tech that could be useful in their quest.

Vendor 6: Raze

Raze was a blacksmith in his former life, now reduced to forging weapons and armor from scavenged materials. Kael's gang demands a hefty cut of his sales, but Raze's skills keep him in business. He is constantly on the lookout for ways to improve his craft and reduce his dependency on Kael's gang. Raze pays 25% of his earnings and provides occasional weapon repairs for Kael's gang.

Protection Money Paid: 25% of earnings and occasional weapon repairs

Table of Products Sold:

Name	Description	Properties	Price
Scrap Weapons	Weapons made from salvaged materials	Standard weapon stats but prone to breaking	10 gp
Scrap Armor	Armor made from scavenged metal	Provides AC but is heavy and cumbersome	15 gp
Weapon Repair Kits	Kits for repairing damaged weapons	Restores durability to damaged weapons	5 gp
Arrow heads	Metal tips for making arrows	Necessary for crafting arrows	2 gp

Information:

Raze has information about a weak point in Kael's defenses that could be exploited for a surprise attack.

He knows that the hidden society in Hope Falls uses advanced technology to maintain their water supply and could potentially provide valuable allies.

Negotiate with Scavenger Leader Kael

Kael is a towering figure, his presence imposing and intimidating. He demands a high price for any assistance or information, and may ask for rare items, significant favors, or a large portion of the party's resources. Negotiating with him requires careful diplomacy or the willingness to make difficult sacrifices.

Negotiation Check: PCs can make a DC 18 Charisma (Persuasion or Deception) check to negotiate a better deal with Kael.

Success: Kael begrudgingly agrees to provide information or assistance for a more reasonable price.

Failure: Kael demands even more, pushing the party to their limits.

Defend Against Kael's Scavengers

After 15 minutes of game time spent negotiating, Kael's Scavengers become more aggressive and suspicious, potentially leading to a confrontation.

Combat: PCs must defend themselves against Kael's Scavengers if negotiations fail or tensions escalate.

Stealth Check: PCs can make a DC 13 Dexterity (Stealth) check to avoid drawing additional attention during their search for pump parts. On a failure, more Scavengers join the fray.

Table of Ruined Buildings in Lost Angeles

Below is a table of buildings and encounters for Lost Angeles. Random results can be rolled with a d20.

1d20	Building Name	Description	Encounter
1	Abandoned Hospital	A crumbling medical facility with decaying equipment and flickering lights.	Encounter with Fungal Hulks in the surgical ward. PCs must avoid toxic spores.
2	Cracked Library	An old library with shelves of moldy, crumbling books and shattered windows.	Mutant Vines have taken over, and PCs must navigate without getting entangled.
3	Fallen Bank	A once-grand bank now reduced to rubble, with a vault still intact.	Sun Blights nest in the vault. PPCs must defeat them to access any remaining valuables.
4	Collapsed School	A school building partially caved in, with classrooms filled with debris.	Scavenger patrol led by a Scavenger captain searching for supplies. PCs can negotiate or fight.
5	Derelict Factory	An old factory with rusting machinery and broken conveyor belts.	Advanced Security Drones still patrol the area. PCs must disable, destroy, or avoid the drones.
6	Haunted Theater	A decrepit theater with torn seats and a broken stage.	Techno-Ghosts haunt the stage area. PCs must confront or appease the ghosts.
7	Ruined Supermarket	A looted supermarket with empty shelves and a faint odor of rot.	PCs encounter a Necrotic Aberration feeding on decaying food. They must defeat it to search safely.
8	Wrecked Apartment	A residential building with collapsed floors and exposed wiring.	A nest of Sun Blights in the upper floors. PCs must clear them to find any useful items.
9	Flooded Basement	The basement of an office building, filled with toxic, stagnant water (upon contact, DC 15 Con save vs poisoned condition for 1 hour).	Mutant Vines grow thick here. PCs must navigate the area without touching the water.
10	Deserted Garage	An auto repair shop with old tools and rusted vehicles.	Scavengers have set up a temporary camp. PCs can trade, negotiate, or fight.
11	Overgrown Park	A public park now overrun with dense, mutated vegetation.	PCs face a group of Fungal Hulks and must solve a puzzle to find a safe path.
12	Ancient Archive	A records office with ancient files and broken filing cabinets.	A trap of automated defenses activates, requiring Technology checks to disable.
13	Abandoned Church	A church with broken stained-glass windows and a crumbling altar.	A Necrotic Aberration resides near the altar, drawn by the site's history.
14	Dilapidated Museum	A museum with shattered display cases and looted exhibits.	Advanced Security Drones protect the remaining artifacts. PCs must disable, destroy, or bypass.
15	Shattered Greenhouse	A greenhouse with broken glass and overgrown plants.	Mutant Vines block the entrance and must be cleared to access the interior.
16	Decayed Subway Station	An underground station filled with debris and stagnant water.	Fungal Hulks have taken residence in the tunnels. PCs must navigate through safely.
17	Crumbling Watchtower	An old watchtower with a view of the city, now partially collapsed.	Scavengers use it as a lookout point. PCs can negotiate or fight to gain control.
18	Rusted Playground	An old playground with rusted equipment and overgrown grass.	Sun Blights nest in the structures. PCs must clear them to make the area safe.
19	Broken Bridge	A bridge over a dry riverbed, now broken and unstable.	Mutant Vines grow across the bridge, making crossing dangerous.
20	Forsaken Police Station	A police station with broken cells and a well-defended Armory containing various old-world weapons.	Advanced Security Drones patrol the area, protecting the Armory.

Terrain

Rubble and Debris: The ground is uneven and filled with obstacles, requiring DC 15 Dexterity (Athletics or Acrobatics) checks to navigate safely.

Collapsing Structures: Buildings and structures are unstable. PCs must make DC 15 Strength (Athletics) or Dexterity (Acrobatics) checks to avoid falling debris and collapsing floors.

Toxic Pools: Any contact with the glowing water requires a DC 15 Constitution saving throw to avoid being poisoned for 1 hour.

Lair Actions

On initiative count 20 (losing initiative ties), the ruined city invokes one of the following lair actions:

Sudden Collapse: A section of a nearby building abruptly collapses. Each creature within a 20-foot radius must make a DC 15 Dexterity saving throw or take 14 (4d6) bludgeoning damage and be knocked prone.

Toxic Gas Release: A pipe bursts, releasing a cloud of toxic gas. Each creature in a 20-foot radius must make a DC 15 Constitution saving throw or be poisoned for 1 minute.

Security System Activation: An old security system suddenly activates, projecting laser grids. Each creature in the area must make a DC 15 Dexterity saving throw or take 12 (3d6) fire damage.

Scaling the Encounter

Beginning Players (PC levels 1-5)

General Adjustments

- Lower the number of hostile creatures in each encounter.
- Reduce DCs for skill checks by 3-5 points.
- Decrease the frequency and intensity of environmental hazards.

Sun Blights

- Keep the number of Sun Blights to 1-2 per encounter.
- Lower their AC to 14 and hit points to 40.

Scavengers: Keep the number of Scavengers to 2-3 per encounter.

Advanced Security Drones

- Lower AC to 12 and hit points to 20.
- Reduce saving throw DCs to 10.

Environmental Hazards

- DCs for navigating rubble and debris: 10
- DCs for avoiding collapsing structures: 10
- DCs for avoiding poison from toxic pools: 10

Intermediate Players (PC levels 6-10)

General Adjustments

- Use standard encounter setups as described.
- Maintain original DCs for skill checks.
- Standard frequency and intensity of environmental hazards.

Sun Blights: Use the preset number of Sun Blights per encounter. Use standard stats.

Scavengers: Keep the number of Scavengers to 4-6 per encounter. Use standard stats.

Advanced Security Drones

- Standard AC (16) and hit points (27).
- Standard saving throw DCs (13).

Environmental Hazards

- DCs for navigating rubble and debris: 15
- DCs for avoiding collapsing structures: 15
- DCs for avoiding poison from toxic pools: 15

Advanced Players (PC levels 11+)

General Adjustments

- Increase the number of hostile creatures in each encounter.
- Raise DCs for skill checks by 2-4 points.
- Increase the frequency and intensity of environmental hazards.

Sun Blights

- Increase the number of Sun Blights to 1d4+2 per encounter.
- Increase AC to 18 and hit points to 100.

Scavengers

- Include multiple Scavengers in larger encounters.
- Increase number and quality of Scavengers.

Advanced Security Drones

- Increase AC to 18 and hit points to 40.
- Increase saving throw DCs to 15.

Environmental Hazards

- DCs for navigating rubble and debris: 17
- DCs for avoiding collapsing structures: 17
- DCs for avoiding poison from toxic pools: 17

Monsters

Sun Blight (1d4+1)

Scavenger (4-6)

Advanced Security Drone (2-3)

Necrotic Aberration

Techno-Ghost

Fungal Hulk

Mutant Vine

NPC

Scavenger Leader Kael: The leader of a powerful Scavenger band who forces local vendors to pay him protection money. He can be negotiated with but demands a high price for any information or assistance.

Hope Falls

The PCs must locate the hidden path to the secluded village of Hope Falls and negotiate with Elder Maren to gain access to the water source. The village employs advanced yet rustic defensive measures to protect itself, presenting both physical and diplomatic challenges for the party.

As you traverse through the dense foliage, the forest suddenly gives way to a serene clearing. Before you lies a thriving village, its collective structures a harmonious blend of ancient stonework and modern technology. Wind turbines and solar panels are interspersed with lush gardens and stone cottages, all centered around a gently flowing stream that feeds into a large water wheel. The wheel turns slowly, and you sense it plays a vital role in the village's operations. Villagers move about their tasks with a sense of purpose, casting wary glances in your direction as you enter.

In the center of the village stands a grand hall, its entrance guarded by two stern-faced sentries. Standing outside, as if expecting your arrival, is an older woman. Her presence commands the area, her silver hair glowing softly in the daylight, and her green eyes studying you with a mix of curiosity and caution. She gestures for you to approach, her movements measured and graceful. This is a place of refuge, but also one of vigilance. You sense that gaining the trust of these people will not be an easy task.

Negotiate with Elder Maren

PCs must use diplomacy to negotiate with Elder Maren and gain her trust. They must prove their intentions and potentially perform tasks for the village to secure access to the water source. This is a crucial point in the party's mission, in which they will need to secure access to the Water Source Facility, obtain and repair a working pump, and utilize the electricity generated from the Water Wheel to power the pump.

Initial Approach

Check: PCs must make an initial DC 15 Charisma (Persuasion) check to present their case to Elder Maren and demonstrate their good intentions.

Outcome:

Success: Elder Maren is cautiously optimistic and willing to listen further. She provides some information about the village and the challenges they face.

Failure: Elder Maren remains skeptical and imposes stricter conditions, requiring additional proof of the PCs' intentions or a higher DC for subsequent checks.

Proving Intentions

Task Assignment: Elder Maren assigns the party a task to prove their intentions and commitment to helping the village. This could involve:

Defending the Village: PCs might need to protect the village from a pending threat, such as an attack by hostile creatures.

Gathering Resources: PCs are sent to collect vital resources or repair materials from a dangerous location.

Healing and Aid: PCs might need to use their skills to heal injured villagers or solve an internal problem.

Check: PCs must complete the assigned task, using relevant skills and abilities. The difficulty and nature of the task depend on the initial negotiation outcome and Elder Maren's assessment of the party.

Securing Access to the Water Source Facility

Check: After completing the task, PCs must make another Charisma (Persuasion) check (DC 18) to secure Elder Maren's approval for accessing the Water Source Facility.

Outcome:

Success: Elder Maren grants access and provides guidance on how to reach and utilize the facility.

Failure: Elder Maren remains hesitant, and PCs may need to complete an additional task or make a higher DC check.

Obtaining and Repairing the Pump

Check: Players may need to further prove their intentions and perhaps demonstrate their technical skills. This can be achieved by repairing a small, damaged water pump found in the village. To repair the small pump, PCs can make an Intelligence (Technology) check using engineer's tools at DC 17.

Outcome:

Success: The small pump is successfully repaired and ready for use.

Failure: PCs must seek additional parts or assistance from village engineers, requiring an additional skill check.

Utilizing the Electricity Generated from the Water Wheel

Check: PCs are asked to integrate the newly repaired small pump with the electricity generated by the Water Wheel. This requires a DC 16 Intelligence (Technology) check using engineer's tools to ensure the connection is stable and efficient.

Outcome:

Success: The pump is successfully powered by the Water Wheel, allowing the water to flow through the Lifeline Pipeline.

Failure: PCs must troubleshoot the connection, requiring additional checks and potentially facing technical issues.

Automated Defense Constructs

Automated Defense Constructs are remnants of advanced technology from the old world, repurposed by the hidden society of Hope Falls to safeguard their village. These constructs vary in size and form, typically resembling humanoid robots or floating drones equipped with non-lethal weaponry. Constructed from durable metals and composite materials, they are designed to withstand harsh environments and repeated use.

Purpose: The primary function of these constructs is to defend key areas within the village, such as the Water Source Facility, the Water Wheel, and important communal structures. They are programmed to detect and respond to potential threats, engaging intruders with non-lethal force to neutralize them without causing permanent harm.

Engagement Tactics

Detection: Automated Defense Constructs are equipped with advanced sensors, allowing them to detect movement, heat signatures, and sound. When an intruder is identified, the construct enters an alert state and moves to intercept.

Non-Lethal Weapons: The constructs are armed with a variety of non-lethal weapons, such as tasers, tranquilizer darts, and stun batons. These weapons are designed to incapacitate intruders rather than kill, rendering them unconscious or immobilized.

Tactical Coordination and Defensive Guards: The constructs can communicate with each other through wireless signals, coordinating their efforts to effectively surround and subdue intruders. They can also alert the human Defensive Guards if additional assistance is required. The Defensive Guards of Hope Falls are highly trained villagers and, like the Automated Defense Constructs, can engage intruders if they are perceived as a threat.

Encounter Mechanics

Stun Dart: *Ranged Weapon Attack:* +5 to hit, range 30/60 ft., one target. *Hit:* 5 (1d8 + 1) piercing damage, and the target must succeed on a DC 13 Constitution saving throw or be paralyzed for 1 minute. The target can repeat the saving throw at the end of each of its turns, ending the effect on itself on a success.

Taser Shock: *Melee Weapon Attack:* +5 to hit, reach 5 ft., one target. *Hit:* 6 (1d6 + 3) lightning damage, and

the target must succeed on a DC 13 Constitution saving throw or be stunned until the end of its next turn.

Tranquilizer Gas: The construct releases a cloud of tranquilizer gas in a 10-foot radius. Each creature in that area must succeed on a DC 13 Constitution saving throw or fall unconscious for 1d4 hours. An unconscious creature wakes up if it takes damage or if another creature uses an action to shake it awake.

Challenge: Automated Defense Constructs present a moderate challenge to intruders. While their non-lethal approach is less deadly than traditional combatants, their ability to incapacitate can turn the tide of an encounter, especially if multiple constructs are involved or if they are supported by human guards. PCs must use strategy and caution to navigate areas protected by these constructs, employing stealth, disabling devices, or negotiating with village authorities to avoid confrontation.

Terrain

The village of Hope Falls is nestled within a dense forest, its pathways winding through ancient trees and overgrown foliage. The ground is mostly even, but roots and underbrush can pose tripping hazards. PCs must make DC 10 Dexterity (Athletics or Acrobatics) checks to avoid these natural obstacles. The bioluminescent fungi provide dim light in some areas, but the deeper parts of the forest are very dark, requiring darkvision or artificial light sources.

Lair Actions

On initiative count 20 (losing initiative ties), Hope Falls invokes one of the following lair actions:

Guardian Traps: The hidden society can activate one of their defensive traps. PCs must make a DC 15 Dexterity saving throw to avoid being caught in a snare or pitfall.

Alarm System: If PCs move suspiciously or cause disturbance, an alarm system may trigger. All PCs must make a DC 15 Wisdom saving throw or become disoriented, giving them disadvantage on their next action.

Barrier Activation: A magical barrier can be activated around a specific area, creating a force field. PCs must make a DC 18 Intelligence (Arcana) check to disable it or find an alternate route.

Scaling The Encounter

Beginning Players (PC levels 1-5)

Engagement Tactics: Use basic stun darts and taser shocks with DC 10-12.

Integrating with Water Wheel: DC 10

- Reduce the complexity of the tasks assigned by Elder Maren (e.g., simple fetch quests or minor village repairs).
- Automated Defense Constructs have lower AC (12) and hit points (20). Reduce their save DCs to 10.

Defensive Guards: Fewer guards with basic equipment and lower hit points.

Intermediate Players (PC levels 6-10)

- Tasks assigned by Elder Maren involve moderate difficulty challenges (e.g., defending the village from minor threats, collecting rare resources).
- Automated Defense Constructs use standard AC (16) and hit points (27). Standard save DCs (13).

Advanced Players (PC levels 11+)

Engagement Tactics: Use tranquilizer gas more strategically, increase damage, and introduce new abilities like area denial.

Automated Defense Constructs have higher AC (18) and hit points (40). Increase their save DCs to 15.

Defensive Guards: Elite guards with high AC, hit points, and additional abilities.

NPC

Elder Maren: The wise and cautious leader of the hidden society, she holds vital information and the key to the water source.

The Water Source Facility

The Water Source Facility is a heavily fortified underground structure where clean water is stored. PCs must secure the water source and defend it against threats, connecting it to water pumps and the Lifeline Pipeline to transport water back across the Wall.

As you descend into the depths of the underground facility, the air becomes cooler and more damp, the walls lined with ancient, corroded metal. The faint hum of machinery can be heard echoing through the corridors, mingling with the occasional drip of water. The tunnels are lit by flickering, dim lights, casting eerie shadows that dance across the rusted walls. As you navigate deeper, the passages widen into a large, open chamber. At the center stands a massive, intricate system of pipes and pumps, their surfaces slick with moisture and age. Pools of clean, shimmering water lie within sight, protected by a series of advanced security systems that still function, albeit erratically.

As you step further into the chamber, you notice the presence of several villagers, their eyes warily tracking your every move. They work diligently, maintaining the ancient machinery with a mix of old and new technology. Suddenly, the ground trembles slightly, and you hear a chittering noise echoing through the facility. Emerging from the shadows, you see several incredibly large, grotesque beetles with thick, armored shells that shimmer with a sickly green hue. Their eyes glow with an unnatural light, and toxic vapor wafts from their bodies. The guards quickly tense up, ready to defend the precious water source from these irradiated invaders.

Defend and Repair

The party must fend off Rad Beetles while simultaneously installing and activating the main pump to restore water flow through the Lifeline Pipeline.

Setup: As the PCs enter the Water Source Facility, they discover that the main pump, a crucial piece of machinery needed to transport water through the Lifeline Pipeline, is missing. The villagers explain that the pump was stolen several months ago by a group of raiders from Lost Angeles. Despite their best efforts, they haven't been able to recover it due to the dangers of venturing into the ruined city.

The theft of the pump is a significant event that ties directly to the PCs' mission in Lost Angeles. The raiders who took it are aware of its value and have moved it to a hidden location within the city, hoping to sell it to the highest bidder. This creates an opportunity for the PCs to potentially recover the original pump instead of finding a replacement, adding an element of choice to their quest.

If the PCs inquire further, some villagers might provide the following information:

- The raiders were seen heading towards the eastern sector of Lost Angeles

- They had a distinctive emblem on their armor: a scarlet scorpion

- Their leader was overheard mentioning a buyer from "the Oasis"

The PCs now have two potential courses of action:

- Secure a replacement pump from elsewhere in Lost Angeles

- Attempt to track down and recover the original stolen pump

Whichever pump they acquire, they still face the challenge of transporting the heavy equipment (weighing 1500 pounds) several miles through the Dumps to the Water Source Facility. They'll need to devise a method to move it safely, connect it to the Lifeline Pipeline, and hook it up to the electricity generated by the Water Wheel.

Throughout this process, Rad Beetles, drawn to the water source, pose a constant threat. The PCs must balance the technical challenges of installing the pump with defending against these irradiated creatures.

Steps to Complete the Activity

Acquire the Pump

If Not Acquired: The party must travel to Lost Angeles to find and retrieve a pump (see separate encounter details for acquiring the pump).

If Acquired: PCs must plan the transportation of the pump to the Water Source Facility.

Transport the Pump

Check: The party must devise a method to move the 1500-pound pump down to the water source.

DC: A DC 15 Intelligence (Technology) check using engineer's tools, possibly using tools like ropes, pulleys, and carts, and a DC 15 Strength (Athletics) check if applicable for manually hauling the pump.

Outcome: Success means the party safely transports the pump without damage. Failure results in delays or potential damage to the pump, requiring repairs (DC 15 Intelligence (Technology) check using engineer's tools).

Connect the Pump

Identify Connections: PCs must determine how to connect the pump to the Lifeline Pipeline and the water source.

DC: A DC 15 Intelligence (Technology) check using engineer's tools.

Outcome: Success correctly connects the pump. Failure causes leaks or misalignment, requiring another check.

Defend Against Rad Beetles

Combat: Rad Beetles attack the party in waves, aiming to disrupt their efforts in a territorial struggle for the water source.

Mechanics: PCs must balance between defending themselves and continuing the installation. Each round, additional Rad Beetles may emerge.

Tactics: Rad Beetles target PCs actively working on the pump first, as the noise of its repair draws their attention.

Activate the Pump

Check: PCs must activate the pump and ensure it is operational by connecting it to the electricity from the Water Wheel.

DC: A DC 15 Intelligence (Technology) check using engineer's tools.

Outcome: Success activates the pump, restoring the flow of water through the Lifeline Pipeline. Failure may cause the pump to malfunction, requiring further repairs.

Combat Mechanics

Wave 1: 2 Rad Beetles emerge from the shadows, targeting the PCs working on the pump.

Wave 2: After 3 rounds, 2 more Rad Beetles appear, adding pressure on the party.

Wave 3: If the pump is not activated within 6 rounds, a final wave of 2 Rad Beetles arrives.

Complications

Interruptions: Each time a PC working on the pump is attacked and hit by a Rad Beetle, they must make a DC 14 Constitution saving throw to maintain their focus. Failure means they lose progress on their current installation action, requiring them to start over.

Environmental Hazards: The facility's unstable structure may occasionally cause debris to fall or machinery to malfunction. The DM can introduce these hazards with a DC 15 Dexterity saving throw to avoid 10 (3d6) bludgeoning damage.

Strategies for Success

Division of Labor: The party should assign roles, with some focusing on installation and others on defense.

Use of Abilities: PCs with spells or abilities that can protect or enhance repair efforts should use them strategically (e.g., using buffs to increase check success rates or shields to protect against attacks).

Resource Management: Ensure that tools and parts are kept safe and accessible, and use healing potions or spells to keep repair-focused PCs in good health.

Rewards

Successful Installation: Ensuring the pump is installed and activated grants the party access to the clean water of the Water Source Facility via the Lifeline Pipeline, vital for their mission to reestablish the water supply to the parched enclave of Utopia and surrounding regions on the other side of the Wall.

Defeating Rad Beetles: Defeating the Rad Beetles provides PCs with valuable resources such as irradiated carapace fragments that can be used for crafting or sold for profit.

Terrain

Slippery Ground: The terrain in the Water Source Facility is damp and slippery, dotted occasionally with pools of water. These slick surfaces require DC 15 Dexterity (Acrobatics) checks to avoid slipping and falling prone.

Cover: Narrow pathways and clusters of machinery provide cover and concealment, granting half cover (+2 to AC and Dexterity saving throws) to those who utilize them.

Lair Actions

On initiative count 20 (losing initiative ties), the Water Source Facility invokes one of the following lair actions:

Radiation Surge: The facility releases a burst of radiation in a 20-foot radius centered on a point within the chamber. Each creature in that area must make a DC 14 Constitution saving throw, taking 7 (2d6) fire damage and 7 (2d6) poison damage on a failed save, or half as much damage on a successful one.

Mechanical Malfunction: A random piece of machinery malfunctions, creating a hazard. Each creature within 10 feet of the malfunctioning machinery must make a DC 15 Dexterity saving throw or take 10 (3d6) bludgeoning damage from flying debris.

Toxic Gas Release: A burst of toxic gas fills a 15-foot radius area. Each creature in that area must succeed on a DC 14 Constitution saving throw or be poisoned for 1 minute. While poisoned in this way, the creature takes 5 (1d10) poison damage at the start of each of its turns.

Scaling The Encounter

Beginning Players (PC levels 1-5)

Defend and Repair

- Reduce the number of Rad Beetles in each wave (1 Rad Beetle per wave).
- Lower the DC for checks:
  - **Transport the Pump**: DC 10
  - **Connect the Pump**: DC 10
  - **Activate the Pump**: DC 10

Environmental hazards occur less frequently and deal less damage (DC 12 Dexterity saving throw, 7 (2d6) bludgeoning damage).

Lair Actions

- **Radiation Surge**: 1d6 fire and 1d6 poison damage, DC 10 Constitution save.
- **Mechanical Malfunction**: 7 (2d6) bludgeoning damage, DC 12 Dexterity save.
- **Toxic Gas Release**: DC 10 Constitution save, 3 (1d6) poison damage per turn.

Intermediate Players (PC levels 6-10)

Defend and Repair

- Maintain the standard number of Rad Beetles in each wave (2 Rad Beetles per wave).
- Use the provided DCs for checks:
  - **Transport the Pump**: DC 15
  - **Connect the Pump**: DC 15
  - **Activate the Pump**: DC 15

Environmental hazards occur with standard frequency and damage (DC 15 Dexterity saving throw, 10 (3d6) bludgeoning damage).

Lair Actions

- **Radiation Surge**: 7 (2d6) fire and 7 (2d6) poison damage, DC 14 Constitution save.
- **Mechanical Malfunction**: 10 (3d6) bludgeoning damage, DC 15 Dexterity save.
- **Toxic Gas Release**: DC 14 Constitution save, 5 (1d10) poison damage per turn.

Advanced Players (PC levels 11+)

Defend and Repair

- Increase the number of Rad Beetles in each wave (3 Rad Beetles per wave).
- Raise the DC for checks:
  - **Transport the Pump**: DC 18
  - **Connect the Pump**: DC 18
  - **Activate the Pump**: DC 18

Environmental hazards occur more frequently and deal more damage (DC 18 Dexterity saving throw, 14 (4d6) bludgeoning damage).

Lair Actions

- **Radiation Surge**: 10 (3d6) fire and 10 (3d6) poison damage, DC 16 Constitution save.
- **Mechanical Malfunction**: 14 (4d6) bludgeoning damage, DC 18 Dexterity save.
- **Toxic Gas Release**: DC 16 Constitution save, 7 (2d6) poison damage per turn.

Monster

Rad Beetle (2)

Conclusions

Conclusions

Triumphant Return

After overcoming numerous challenges, the PCs successfully restore the Lifeline Pipeline and secure a stable water source for their homeland. The once-desolate enclave begins to flourish, and the PCs return to Utopia as celebrated heroes.

As you approach the gates of Utopia, the sight of your enclave fills you with a renewed sense of hope. The once dry and cracked ground now shows signs of life, with green shoots emerging where there was only dust. People gather at the gates, their faces lighting up as they see you. Cheers erupt from the crowd and children run ahead to greet you, their laughter a stark contrast to the somber silence that once dominated this place.

You are ushered into the heart of the enclave where Commander Rylan waits, a rare smile breaking his stern demeanor. "You did it," he says, his voice filled with admiration. "Thanks to you, we have a future." The celebration that follows is filled with joy and gratitude, as the people of Utopia come together to honor your bravery and ingenuity. The lifeblood of your home flows freely once more, and with it, the promise of prosperity and growth.

Rewards

Hero's Feast: The party is treated to a grand feast, replenishing their strength and lifting their spirits. Each PC gains temporary hit points equal to their level + 10, and advantage on all saving throws for the next 24 hours.

Medals of Valor: Each PC is awarded a Medal of Valor, a symbol of their bravery and accomplishment. This medal grants a +1 bonus to all Charisma-based skill checks when dealing with members of Utopia and other allied enclaves of the Walled Territories.

Resource Allocation: As heroes of the enclave, the PCs receive priority access to resources. This includes a weekly stipend of rations and supplies worth 50 gp, and free repairs and upgrades to their equipment for the next month.

Land and Title: EachPC is granted a plot of land within Utopia, along with the title of Protector. This land can be developed into a home or workshop, providing a base of operations and a permanent safe haven.

Ancient Relic: As a token of appreciation, Commander Rylan presents the party with an ancient relic that was recently discovered during the excavation of the pipeline. This relic can be a magical item of the DM's choice, appropriate to the party's level and useful for future adventures.

Pyrrhic Victory

The party succeeds in activating the Lifeline Pipeline, but the victory comes at a great cost. Several party members are lost or severely injured, and the water source is less abundant than hoped, resulting in mixed feelings upon their return to Utopia.

As you approach the gates of Utopia, the familiar sight of home brings a mixture of relief and sorrow. Water now flows through the once-dry ground, but the flow is intermittent and less stable than hoped for. The people of Utopia gather to greet you, their expressions a blend of gratitude and concern as they notice your injuries and weary faces.

Commander Rylan steps forward, his usual stern expression softened by a hint of sadness. "You have done more than we could ever ask," he says, his voice heavy with emotion. "But I see the toll it has taken on you, and the challenges that still lie ahead."

As the enclave celebrates the return of their heroes and the promise of water, there is an underlying current of quiet concern. The journey has left its mark on your bodies and spirits, and the Lifeline Pipeline, while functional, requires constant maintenance due to years of neglect and damage. The water flow is inconsistent, requiring careful rationing and ongoing repairs.

The victory, while significant, has revealed the true scope of the task ahead. Utopia now faces the challenge of maintaining and improving the fragile water system, all while defending it from those who would seek to control this precious resource.

Rewards

Healing and Recovery: The PCs receive immediate medical attention, ensuring that their injuries are treated. Each PC regains hit points equal to half their maximum hit points and gains advantage on all saving throws against diseases and poison for the next week.

Commendation of Sacrifice: Each PC is awarded a Commendation of Sacrifice, recognizing their bravery and the high cost of their victory. This commendation grants a +1 bonus to all Wisdom-based skill checks when interacting with members of Utopia, as a symbol of their deep understanding and resilience.

Resource Support: Despite the limited water supply, the PCs are given priority access to rations and medical supplies. Each PC receives a monthly stipend of supplies worth 25 gp and access to the enclave's best healers for the next three months.

Title of Endurance: Each PC is granted the title of Endurer, acknowledging their perseverance and strength. This title comes with a plot of land within Utopia and the right to call upon the community for support in times of need, reflecting the deep bonds forged through their sacrifice.

Mystical Relic: As a gesture of gratitude, Commander Rylan presents the party with a mystical relic recently found near the pipeline. This relic is a minor magical item of the DM's choice, providing a small but significant benefit to the party, such as increased resistance to environmental hazards or a limited ability to purify water.

Bitter Defeat

The party's mission to secure the water source ends in failure. They return to their enclave with heavy hearts, aware that their people will continue to struggle for survival. This sets the stage for future quests and challenges as they seek alternative solutions.

You make your way back to Utopia, the weight of failure pressing heavily on your shoulders. The journey back feels longer than before, each step a reminder of the water you couldn't bring home. As you pass through the gates, the familiar faces of your fellow citizens are marred with worry and anticipation.

Commander Rylan meets your gaze, his expression stern but understanding. "You've done all you could," he says, his voice steady yet filled with unspoken disappointment. The enclave gathers around, their hopes visibly dimmed by your return without the promised water. Despite your best efforts, the struggle for survival continues. The air is thick with a sense of shared loss, but also with a silent resolve to keep fighting. Your journey is not over; it is only the beginning of a greater quest to save your home.

Rewards

Acknowledgment of Effort: Each PC receives an Acknowledgment of Effort token from Commander Rylan. This token symbolizes their bravery and dedication, granting a +1 bonus to Charisma-based skill checks within Utopia as a mark of their respected status.

Survival Supplies: Despite the failure, the enclave provides each PC with essential survival supplies. Each character receives a survival kit containing rations, water purification tablets, and basic medical supplies worth 50 gp, to aid them in their next quest.

Strategic Planning Session: The PCs are invited to a strategic planning session with the enclave's leaders. This session provides valuable insight and information about potential new quests, granting the PCs advantage on Intelligence (Investigation) checks related to future missions.

Resolve of the Fallen: The PCs are given a relic known as the Resolve of the Fallen, a symbol of their unyielding spirit. This relic allows each PC to reroll one failed saving throw once per long rest, embodying the determination to overcome future challenges.

Unforeseen Consequences

The party successfully activates the Lifeline Pipeline, bringing much-needed water to Utopia. However, this success attracts the attention of marauding groups in the Wasteland, who now see the water supply as a valuable target. The PCs must prepare to defend their enclave from these new threats, setting the stage for further adventures.

As the Lifeline Pipeline roars to life, water flows through the ancient channels and into Utopia, bringing hope and relief to your people. Cheers erupt around you as the once-dry fountains and wells begin to overflow. The joy of your success, however, is short-lived. Scouts report that the sight of the water has drawn the attention of marauding groups lurking in the Wasteland.

Commander Rylan addresses you with a grim expression. "We've secured the water, but now we must secure our home," he says. "Our success has painted a target on our backs. These marauders will come, and we must be ready to defend what we've worked so hard to achieve."

The air in Utopia is charged with both celebration and tension. Your journey is far from over; new challenges await as you prepare to protect your enclave from those who would take it by force. The survival of your community depends on your strength and strategy in the battles to come.

Rewards

Defensive Upgrades: Each PC receives a set of fortified armor, or weapons specifically designed to help defend Utopia. This gear grants a +1 bonus to AC or attack/damage rolls and is tailored for defensive strategies.

Leadership Recognition: The enclave's leadership bestows upon each PC a Medal of Valor, symbolizing their role in securing the water supply. This medal grants advantage on Charisma (Persuasion) and Charisma (Intimidation) checks when dealing with Utopia's residents and allies.

Strategic Resources: PCs are given access to Utopia's newly established Resource Depot, where they can acquire additional supplies for their defenses. Each PC receives a stipend of 100 gp worth of defensive supplies, such as barricades, traps, and fortifications.

Tactical Training: The PCs undergo advanced tactical training with Utopia's military leaders, gaining new insights into defensive warfare. This training grants each character proficiency in one new weapon or armor type of their choice, reflecting their preparation for the coming battles.

Guardian's Favor: As a token of appreciation, the party receives the Guardian's Favor, a magical amulet that can be activated once per long rest to cast the spell *Shield of Faith* (+2 to AC for 10 minutes) on the wearer. This amulet symbolizes their role as protectors of Utopia and will aid them in future confrontations.

A Darker Path

The party decides to hoard the water from the Lifeline Pipeline, choosing to create their own community where they can profit by bartering and selling this precious resource. This decision comes with severe consequences: the people of Utopia will likely die from lack of water, and the PCs become targets for other communities that now see them as a valuable but hated community.

As the water begins to flow through the Lifeline Pipeline, a different plan forms in your minds. Instead of sharing this precious resource with Utopia, you decide to claim it for yourselves. With this water, you can create your own community, one that thrives on the wealth and power that water will bring in this barren world.

You watch as the first few gallons of water gush forth, a symbol of your newfound control. The people of Utopia, once hopeful, now face a grim future without the water you promised. You leave the enclave behind, carrying the knowledge and means to establish a stronghold where water is your currency.

However, this path is fraught with danger. As news of your control over the water supply spreads, you become the target of envy and hatred from other communities. Civil settlements and wild bands alike view you as both a threat and a prize, ready to take what you have claimed for themselves by any means necessary.

You must now prepare for the constant threats that this dark decision has invited. The stakes have never been higher, and the cost of your ambition may be more than you ever imagined.

Rewards

Waterlord's Regalia: Each PC receives a set of luxurious gear befitting their new status as rulers of the water supply. This gear grants a +1 bonus to AC and Charisma (Persuasion) checks, emphasizing their newfound authority and wealth.

Wealth and Supplies: The PCs start their new community with a significant stockpile of goods. Each character receives 500 gp worth of trade goods, rare materials, and survival supplies, reflecting their initial gains from hoarding the water.

Elite Guard: To protect their new stronghold, the PCs are granted a small group of elite guards. These NPCs are loyal to the party and skilled in combat, providing additional security and assistance in future encounters.

Water-Infused Artifacts: EachPC receives a magical item that harnesses the power of the water they control. Examples include a Ring of Water Walking, a Decanter of Endless Water, or a Wand of Water Breathing. These items symbolize their dominion over water and grant practical benefits.

Fortified Stronghold: The PCs establish a well-defended base of operations, equipped with state-of-the-art defenses and comforts. This stronghold provides a safe haven and strategic advantage, granting the PCs advantage on Intelligence (Investigation) and Wisdom (Perception) checks made to fortify and defend their new territory.

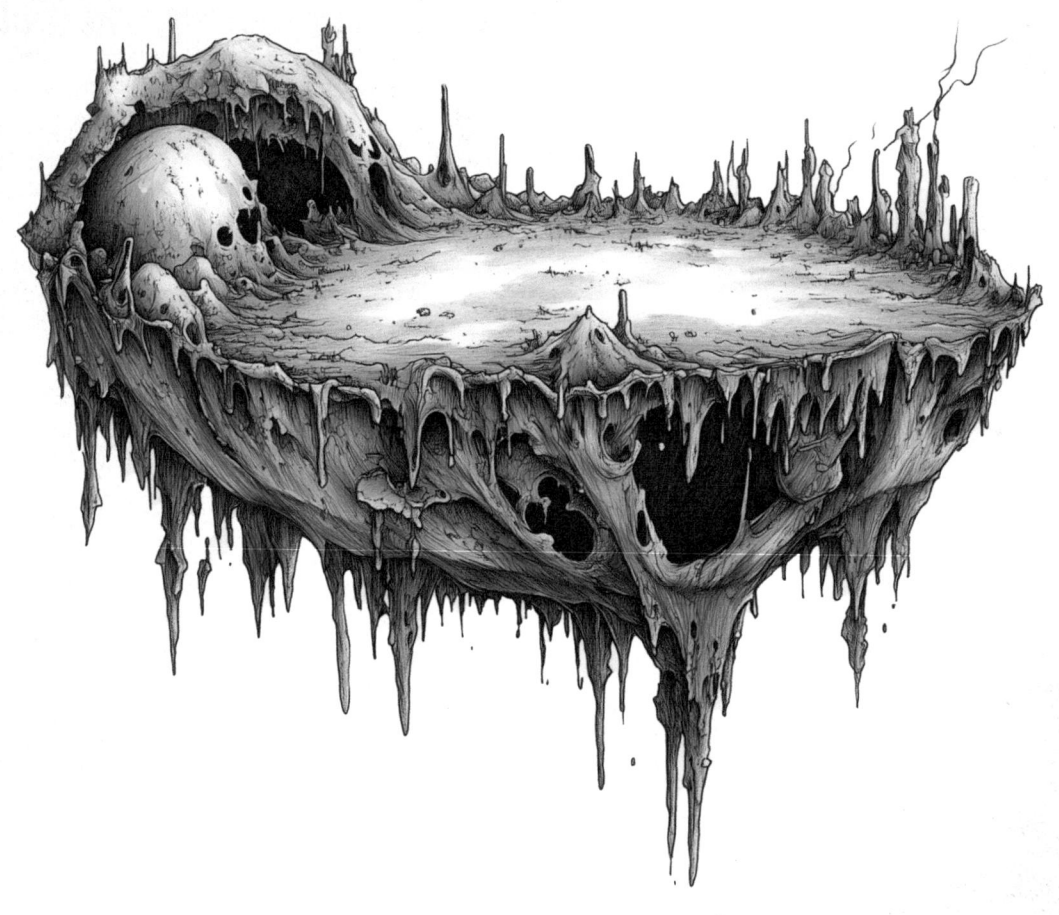

Monsters

Monsters

Advanced Security Drone

Small construct, unaligned

Armor Class: 16 (natural armor)

Hit Points: 27 (5d6 + 10)

Speed: 0 ft., fly 30 ft. (hover)

STR	DEX	CON	INT	WIS	CHA
10 (+0)	14 (+2)	14 (+2)	10 (+0)	10 (+0)	1 (-5)

Damage Immunities: poison, psychic

Condition Immunities: charmed, exhaustion, frightened, paralyzed, petrified, poisoned

Senses: darkvision 60 ft., passive Perception 10

Languages: Understands commands in Common but can't speak

Challenge: 1 (200 XP)

Actions

Laser Beam: *Ranged Weapon Attack:* +4 to hit, range 60 ft., one target. *Hit:* 7 (1d8 + 2) fire damage.

Taser Shock: *Melee Weapon Attack:* +4 to hit, reach 5 ft., one target. *Hit:* 5 (1d6 + 2) lightning damage and the target must succeed on a DC 13 Constitution saving throw or be stunned until the end of its next turn.

Description

Advanced Security Drones are sleek, metallic constructs about the size of a small dog. They hover silently, their smooth, rounded bodies devoid of any unnecessary protrusions. Their surfaces are marked with faint glowing lines that pulse with energy, indicating their active status. These drones are equipped with a single, unblinking sensor eye that scans the area for intruders, and their underside houses retractable appendages for laser beams and taser shocks.

Created by pre-apocalyptic engineers to guard vital installations, Advanced Security Drones were once the pinnacle of automated defense technology. Programmed with a simple directive to neutralize any unauthorized entities, these drones have continued their watch long after their creators have perished. They patrol ancient ruins and forgotten facilities, their advanced AI systems allowing them to operate independently. While they cannot communicate verbally, they can understand commands given in Common, making them a potential asset for those who can hack or reprogram them. However, their unwavering loyalty to their original purpose makes them formidable adversaries for any who dare trespass into their domains.

Dune Drake

Small dragon, chaotic neutral

Armor Class: 15 (natural armor)

Hit Points: 66 (12d6 + 24)

Speed: 30 ft., fly 60 ft.

STR	DEX	CON	INT	WIS	CHA
14 (+2)	18 (+4)	14 (+2)	10 (+0)	12 (+1)	14 (+2)

Saving Throws: Dex +7, Con +5, Wis +4, Cha +5

Skills: Perception +7, Stealth +7, Survival +4

Damage Immunities: fire

Senses: darkvision 60 ft., passive Perception 17

Languages: Draconic

Challenge: 4 (1,100 XP)

Flyby. The drake doesn't provoke opportunity attacks when it flies out of an enemy's reach.

Territorial Instinct. The drake has advantage on attack rolls against creatures within 30 feet of its nest or territory.

Actions

Multiattack. The drake makes two attacks: one with its bite and one with its claws.

Bite. *Melee Weapon Attack:* +5 to hit, reach 5 ft., one target. *Hit:* 9 (2d6 + 2) piercing damage.

Claws. *Melee Weapon Attack:* +5 to hit, reach 5 ft., one target. *Hit:* 7 (1d8 + 3) slashing damage.

Fire Breath (Recharge 5-6). The drake exhales fire in a 15-foot cone. Each creature in that area must make a DC 13 Dexterity saving throw, taking 24 (7d6) fire damage on a failed save, or half as much damage on a successful one.

Description

Dune Drakes are small, agile draconic creatures with scales that shimmer like desert sand. They have slender, aerodynamic bodies, perfect for gliding through the arid air. Their wings are broad and leathery, with a wingspan of about 10 feet, and are equipped with small, clawed digits. The drakes' eyes are a piercing yellow, with slit pupils that give them a predatory look. Their scales range in color from golden brown to deep amber, allowing them to blend seamlessly with their sandy surroundings. Sharp claws and teeth, along with a ridge of spines running down their backs, make them formidable opponents despite their small size.

Dune Drakes are elusive and fiercely territorial creatures that inhabit the vast deserts of the Wasteland. These dragon-like beings are known for their incredible speed and agility, often seen gliding effortlessly through the desert air, scouting for intruders. Highly protective of their nesting areas, Dune Drakes will aggressively defend their territory from any perceived threats. They have an innate ability to breathe fire, a trait that has led many to believe they are descendants of true dragons. Legends among the desert tribes tell of the drakes' cunning and intelligence, with some even claiming that the drakes have a rudimentary form of language. The harsh environment of the desert has honed their survival instincts, making them adept hunters and fierce combatants. Despite their ferocity, there are tales of rare alliances formed between the drakes and those who respect their domain, hinting at a deeper, more complex nature than mere beasts.

Fungal Hulk

Large humanoid (plant), neutral evil

Armor Class: 14 (natural armor)

Hit Points: 95 (10d10 + 40)

Speed: 20 ft.

STR	DEX	CON	INT	WIS	CHA
20 (+5)	8 (-1)	18 (+4)	6 (-2)	12 (+1)	6 (-2)

Saving Throws: Str +8, Con +7, Wis +4

Skills: Perception +4, Survival +4

Damage Resistances: poison; bludgeoning, piercing, and slashing from nonmagical attacks

Condition Immunities: charmed, frightened, poisoned

Senses: darkvision 60 ft., passive Perception 14

Languages: Understands Common but can't speak

Challenge: 6 (2,300 XP)

Toxic Spores. Any creature that starts its turn within 10 feet of the Fungal Hulk must succeed on a DC 15 Constitution saving throw or be poisoned until the start of its next turn. While poisoned in this way, the creature experiences vivid hallucinations.

Regeneration. The Fungal Hulk regains 10 hit points at the start of its turn if it has at least 1 hit point and isn't in sunlight. If the Fungal Hulk takes fire damage, this trait doesn't function at the start of its next turn.

Actions

Multiattack. The Fungal Hulk makes two Slam attacks.

Slam. *Melee Weapon Attack:* +8 to hit, reach 5 ft., one target. *Hit:* 15 (2d8 + 6) bludgeoning damage.

Spore Burst (Recharge 5-6). The Fungal Hulk releases a burst of toxic spores in a 20-foot radius. Each creature in that area must make a DC 15 Constitution saving throw, taking 21 (6d6) poison damage on a failed save, or half as much damage on a successful one. A creature that fails the saving throw is also poisoned for 1 minute. The poisoned creature can repeat the saving throw at the end of each of its turns, ending the effect on itself on a

success.

Description

Fungal Hulks are towering, humanoid figures, standing around 8 feet tall and covered in a thick layer of glowing, toxic fungi. Their skin, if it can still be called that, is a mix of mottled green and brown, overgrown with bioluminescent mushrooms and spongy mold. The faint glow from the fungi casts eerie shadows on their massive frames. Their eyes are sunken pits, barely visible beneath the fungal growths, and their movements are slow but powerful. The air around them is filled with a faint, sickly-sweet smell of decay and spores.

Fungal Hulks are the tragic result of humans or other humanoids succumbing to the pervasive fungal infestations of the Wasteland. Once living beings, they have been overtaken by the toxic fungi, their bodies transformed into lumbering behemoths driven by a primal urge to spread their spores. These creatures are often found in dark, damp environments where the fungi thrive, such as abandoned ruins or dense forests. The spores they emit are highly toxic, causing vivid hallucinations and madness in those who inhale them. Despite their slow movements, Fungal Hulks possess immense strength and can regenerate from most wounds, making them formidable adversaries. The origins of the fungi that create these hulks are shrouded in mystery, with some believing they are the result of ancient, arcane experiments gone awry. Others whisper of a malevolent force behind the fungi, using the hulks as pawns in a larger, more sinister plan. Regardless of their origins, Fungal Hulks are a constant threat in the Wasteland, embodying the relentless and transformative power of nature's darker side.

Guardian Sentinel

Large construct, lawful neutral

Armor Class: 18 (natural armor)

Hit Points: 142 (15d10 + 60)

Speed: 30 ft.

STR	DEX	CON	INT	WIS	CHA
20 (+5)	12 (+1)	18 (+4)	10 (+0)	14 (+2)	6 (-2)

Saving Throws: Str +9, Con +8, Wis +6

Damage Resistances: fire, lightning; bludgeoning, piercing, and slashing from nonmagical attacks

Damage Immunities: poison, psychic

Condition Immunities: charmed, exhaustion, frightened, paralyzed, petrified, poisoned

Senses: darkvision 60 ft., passive Perception 12

Languages: Understands Common and Binary but can't speak

Challenge: 9 (5,000 XP)

Immutable Form. The Guardian Sentinel is immune to any spell or effect that would alter its form.

Magic Resistance. The Guardian Sentinel has advantage on saving throws against spells and other magical effects.

Actions

Multiattack. The Guardian Sentinel makes three attacks: two with its laser cannon and one with its energy blade.

Laser Cannon. *Ranged Weapon Attack:* +9 to hit, range 60/240 ft., one target. *Hit:* 18 (3d8 + 5) fire damage.

Energy Blade. *Melee Weapon Attack:* +9 to hit, reach 10 ft., one target. *Hit:* 15 (2d8 + 6) lightning damage.

Overcharge (Recharge 5-6). The Guardian Sentinel releases a burst of energy in a 30-foot radius. Each creature in that area must make a DC 16 Dexterity saving throw, taking 42 (12d6) force damage on a failed save, or half as much damage on a successful one.

Reactive Shielding. When the Guardian Sentinel is hit by an attack, it can use its reaction to gain a +5 bonus to AC until the start of its next turn, including against the triggering attack.

Description

Guardian Sentinels are imposing constructs, standing nearly 10 feet tall with a broad, humanoid frame crafted from a combination of sleek metal alloys and advanced composite materials. Their surface is adorned with intricate engravings and glowing runes that pulse with a soft, blue light. The sentinels' eyes are twin orbs of radiant energy, scanning their surroundings with an unwavering gaze. Their right arm is equipped with a formidable laser cannon, while their left arm houses a retractable energy blade. The overall design is both elegant and intimidating, reflecting the pinnacle of pre-apocalypse engineering.

Guardian Sentinels are ancient robots created by the pre-apocalypse civilization to serve as protectors and enforcers. These sentinels were programmed with advanced artificial intelligence to recognize and eliminate any perceived threats, ensuring the safety and stability of the society that built them. However, after the Catastrophe, many of these constructs were left to operate autonomously, following their last directives with unwavering dedication.

Over the centuries, the Guardian Sentinels have become relics of a bygone era, continuing their patrols and duties in the ruins of the old world. They are often found in abandoned cities, research facilities, and ancient fortresses, tirelessly guarding the remnants of their creators. Their sophisticated programming and formidable weaponry make them formidable adversaries, and they respond to intruders with lethal precision. Despite their current isolation, some believe that reactivating and reprogramming a Guardian Sentinel could provide invaluable assistance in the harsh Wasteland. However, gaining control over one of these ancient protectors is no small feat, requiring both technical expertise and a deep understanding of their intricate systems.

Mutant Hound

Medium monstrosity, chaotic neutral

Armor Class: 14 (natural armor)

Hit Points: 45 (6d8 + 18)

Speed: 40 ft.

STR	DEX	CON	INT	WIS	CHA
16 (+3)	14 (+2)	16 (+3)	3 (-4)	14 (+2)	6 (-2)

Skills: Perception +6, Stealth +4, Survival +4

Senses: darkvision 60 ft., passive Perception 16

Languages: Understands Common but can't speak

Challenge: 3 (700 XP)

Keen Smell. The hound has advantage on Wisdom (Perception) checks that rely on smell.

Pack Tactics. The hound has advantage on an attack roll against a creature if at least one of the hound's allies is within 5 feet of the creature and the ally isn't incapacitated.

Savage Bite. If the hound hits a creature with a bite attack, the target must succeed on a DC 13 Constitution saving throw or be afflicted with a minor poison that causes disadvantage on its next attack roll or ability check.

Actions

Multiattack. The hound makes two attacks: one with its bite and one with its claws.

Bite. *Melee Weapon Attack:* +5 to hit, reach 5 ft., one target. *Hit:* 10 (2d6 + 3) piercing damage.

Claws. *Melee Weapon Attack:* +5 to hit, reach 5 ft., one target. *Hit:* 8 (1d8 + 3) slashing damage.

Description

Mutant Hounds are grotesque and fearsome creatures, standing slightly taller than a normal dog with a more muscular and contorted frame. Their fur is patchy and matted, revealing patches of leathery, scarred skin. Their eyes glow with a sickly yellow light, and their mouths are filled with jagged, uneven teeth, some of which protrude from their lips. Their claws are elongated and razor-sharp, perfect for rending flesh. The hounds move

with an unsettling mix of agility and brute force, their heightened senses constantly on high alert.

Mutant Hounds are the result of the harsh environmental conditions and exposure to toxic substances that have plagued the Wasteland for generations. Once ordinary wild dogs, these creatures have evolved—or rather, devolved—into aggressive and highly efficient predators. Their keen senses make them excellent trackers, and their pack mentality allows them to coordinate attacks with deadly precision. Tales from survivors speak of the hounds' near-unbreakable loyalty to their pack leader, often a particularly large and fearsome hound. These creatures are a constant threat to those who venture into the Wasteland, their presence often heralded by eerie howls carried on the wind. Despite their terrifying appearance and behavior, some believe that the Mutant Hounds are simply doing what they must to survive in a world that has become increasingly hostile and unforgiving.

Mutant Vine

Large plant, unaligned

Armor Class: 13 (natural armor)

Hit Points: 85 (10d10 + 30)

Speed: 0 ft.

STR	DEX	CON	INT	WIS	CHA
18 (+4)	10 (+0)	16 (+3)	1 (-5)	12 (+1)	3 (-4)

Damage Resistances: bludgeoning, piercing

Damage Immunities: poison

Condition Immunities: blinded, deafened, exhaustion, prone

Senses: blindsight 60 ft., passive Perception 11

Languages: --

Challenge: 6 (2,300 XP)

Actions

Multiattack. The Mutant Vine makes two Vine Lash attacks.

Vine Lash. *Melee Weapon Attack:* +7 to hit, reach 15 ft., one target. *Hit:* 15 (2d10 + 4) bludgeoning damage and the target is grappled (escape DC 15). Until this grapple ends, the target is restrained, and the Mutant Vine can't use this vine stem on another target.

Crush. The Mutant Vine can use its action to deal 21 (6d6) bludgeoning damage to a creature grappled by it.

Entangling Vines (Recharge 5-6). The Mutant Vine targets a point on the ground within 30 feet. Multiple vine stems erupt from the ground in a 20-foot radius centered on that point. Each creature in that area must succeed on a DC 15 Strength saving throw or be restrained. A restrained creature can use its action to make a DC 15 Strength check, freeing itself on a success. The vines wither away after 1 minute.

Poisonous Thorns. Any creature that takes damage from the Mutant Vine must succeed on a DC 15 Constitution saving throw or be poisoned for 1 minute. While poisoned in this way, the creature takes 5 (1d10) poison damage at the start of each of its turns. The creature can repeat the saving throw at the end of each of its turns, ending the effect on itself on a success.

Description

Mutant Vines are a grotesque and menacing sight, a mass of writhing, dark green tendrils that seem to pulse with a life of their own. These vines are covered in thick, razor-sharp thorns that glisten with a toxic sap. Their movements are unnervingly fluid, almost serpentine, as they reach out to ensnare anything that comes too close. At their core, the vines are anchored to a bulbous, root-like mass that seems to feed on the nutrients of whatever unfortunate creatures fall prey to them. The air around the Mutant Vine is filled with a faint, sickly-sweet odor, hinting at the deadly poison it exudes.

Mutant Vines are the result of the Wasteland's extreme conditions, having evolved from ordinary plant life into carnivorous predators. These monstrous plants have adapted to their harsh environment by developing a variety of deadly traits. They lie in wait, often camouflaged among other vegetation, ready to strike at anything that ventures too close. The thorns of the Mutant Vine are not only capable of inflicting severe wounds but also inject a potent toxin that weakens and eventually kills its prey.

Legends among the Wasteland's survivors speak of entire groups being consumed by these ravenous plants, their remains slowly decomposed and absorbed by the vines. Despite their danger, some believe that the toxins and other compounds produced by the Mutant Vines hold valuable properties, potentially useful for crafting

powerful poisons or antidotes. However, harvesting such materials is an extremely perilous task, one that few dare to undertake. The existence of Mutant Vines serves as a grim reminder of nature's ability to adapt and thrive, even in the most inhospitable of environments.

Necrotic Aberration

Large undead, chaotic evil

Armor Class: 16 (natural armor)

Hit Points: 120 (16d10 + 32)

Speed: 30 ft.

STR	DEX	CON	INT	WIS	CHA
18 (+4)	10 (+0)	18 (+4)	7 (-2)	14 (+2)	12 (+1)

Saving Throws: Con +8, Wis +6, Cha +5

Damage Resistances: cold, necrotic; bludgeoning, piercing, and slashing from nonmagical attacks

Damage Immunities: poison

Condition Immunities: charmed, exhaustion, frightened, paralyzed, poisoned

Senses: darkvision 60 ft., passive Perception 12

Languages: Understands Common but can't speak

Challenge: 8 (3,900 XP)

Aura of Death. Any creature that starts its turn within 10 feet of the Necrotic Aberration must succeed on a DC 16 Constitution saving throw or take 10 (3d6) necrotic damage and have its hit point maximum reduced by an amount equal to the necrotic damage taken. This reduction lasts until the target finishes a long rest. The target dies if this effect reduces its hit point maximum to 0.

Regeneration. The Necrotic Aberration regains 10 hit points at the start of its turn if it has at least 1 hit point.

Undead Fortitude. If damage reduces the Necrotic Aberration to 0 hit points, it must make a Constitution saving throw with a DC of 5 + the damage taken, unless the damage is radiant or from a critical hit. On a success, the Necrotic Aberration drops to 1 hit point instead.

Actions

Multiattack. The Necrotic Aberration makes two claw attacks.

Claw. *Melee Weapon Attack:* +8 to hit, reach 5 ft., one target. Hit: 15 (2d8 + 6) slashing damage plus 7 (2d6) necrotic damage.

Necrotic Drain (Recharge 5-6). The Necrotic Aberration targets one creature it can see within 30 feet. The target must make a DC 16 Constitution saving throw, taking 35 (10d6) necrotic damage on a failed save, or half as much damage on a successful one. The Necrotic Aberration regains hit points equal to half the damage dealt.

Description

Necrotic Aberrations are terrifying amalgamations of decayed flesh and mutated tissue, standing at about 8 feet tall. Their bodies are a gruesome patchwork of decomposing flesh, bone, and sinew, held together by dark, pulsating veins. Their skin is a mottled gray-green, covered in patches of rot and festering wounds. Eyes of various shapes and sizes, all clouded and lifeless, are scattered haphazardly across their bodies. They exude a palpable aura of death, the air around them heavy with the stench of decay. Their claws are elongated and sharp, dripping with a black ichor that seems to absorb the light.

Necrotic Aberrations are the horrifying result of dark necromantic experiments and the lingering curses of the old world. These creatures are formed from the remains of countless dead, stitched together by vile magic and animated with a malevolent will. They are often found in the darkest and most cursed places of the Wasteland, drawn to areas of death and decay. Legends among survivors speak of powerful necromancers who created these abominations as guardians of their forbidden secrets or as weapons of terror.

The Necrotic Aberrations' ability to drain the life force of those nearby makes them particularly feared. Their presence alone can weaken even the strongest of warriors, and their touch is death itself. Despite their grotesque appearance and mindless nature, there is a tragic aspect to their existence; the souls of the many who comprise their form are said to be trapped in eternal torment, unable to find peace. Some believe that destroying a Necrotic Aberration can release these souls, granting them the rest they so desperately crave. However, facing such a creature is a perilous endeavor, one that few undertake lightly.

Rad Beetle

Large monstrosity, unaligned

Armor Class: 17 (natural armor)

Hit Points: 85 (10d10 + 30)

Speed: 30 ft.

STR	DEX	CON	INT	WIS	CHA
18 (+4)	10 (+0)	16 (+3)	3 (-4)	12 (+1)	5 (-3)

Saving Throws: Con +6, Dex +3

Skills: Perception +4

Damage Resistances: acid, poison; bludgeoning, piercing, and slashing from nonmagical attacks

Senses: darkvision 60 ft., passive Perception 14

Languages: --

Challenge: 6 (2,300 XP)

Toxic Aura. Any creature that starts its turn within 10 feet of the Rad Beetle must succeed on a DC 14 Constitution saving throw or take 7 (2d6) poison damage and be poisoned until the start of its next turn.

Tough Shell. The Rad Beetle has advantage on saving throws against spells and other magical effects.

Actions

Multiattack. The Rad Beetle makes two attacks: one with its bite and one with its acid spray.

Bite. *Melee Weapon Attack:* +7 to hit, reach 5 ft., one target. *Hit:* 13 (2d8 + 4) piercing damage.

Acid Spray. *Ranged Weapon Attack:* +7 to hit, range 30/60 ft., one target. *Hit:* 16 (3d10) acid damage.

Irradiated Burst (Recharge 5-6). The Rad Beetle releases a burst of radiation in a 20-foot radius. Each creature in that area must make a DC 14 Constitution saving throw, taking 14 (4d6) fire damage and 14 (2d6)

poison damage on a failed save, or half as much damage on a successful one. A creature that fails the saving throw is also poisoned for 1 minute. A poisoned creature can repeat the saving throw at the end of each of its turns, ending the effect on itself on a success.

Description

Rad Beetles are enormous, grotesque creatures, roughly the size of a large horse, with thick, armored shells that shimmer with a sickly green hue. Their eyes are small, beady, and glow with an unnatural light, hinting at the radiation coursing through their bodies. The Rad Beetle's mandibles are jagged and strong, capable of crushing bone with ease. Patches of their shell occasionally emit faint wisps of toxic vapor, and their movements are accompanied by a low, ominous hum.

Rad Beetles are a terrifying result of the Wasteland's irradiated environment, having mutated from ordinary beetles into formidable and dangerous creatures. Their bodies have adapted to not only withstand but thrive in high levels of radiation, which they can weaponize against their enemies. These beetles are often found near sources of radiation, scavenging for food and nesting in the ruins of the old world. Their toxic aura and ability to spray acid make them a significant threat to any who encounter them, while their tough shells provide substantial protection. Stories among survivors tell of entire scavenging parties falling prey to a single Rad Beetle, their bodies left to decay in the irradiated wastelands. Despite their fearsome reputation, some daring (or desperate) individuals seek out these creatures, believing their irradiated remains hold untapped potential for crafting powerful items or as a source of energy.

Scavenger

Medium humanoid (human), chaotic neutral

Armor Class: 14 (leather armor)

Hit Points: 52 (8d8 + 16)

Speed: 30 ft.

STR	DEX	CON	INT	WIS	CHA
16 (+3)	14 (+2)	14 (+2)	10 (+0)	12 (+1)	10 (+0)

Saving Throws: Str +5, Con +4

Skills: Athletics +5, Intimidation +4, Perception +3, Stealth +4

Senses: darkvision 60 ft., passive Perception 13

Languages: Common, Thieves' Cant

Challenge: 3 (700 XP)

Brute. A melee weapon deals one extra die of its damage when the Scavenger hits with it (included in the attack).

Pack Tactics. The Scavenger has advantage on an attack roll against a creature if at least one of the Scavenger's allies is within 5 feet of the creature and the ally isn't incapacitated.

Actions

Multiattack. The Scavenger makes two melee attacks.

Scimitar. *Melee Weapon Attack:* +5 to hit, reach 5 ft., one target. *Hit:* 10 (2d6 + 3) slashing damage.

Heavy Crossbow. *Ranged Weapon Attack:* +4 to hit, range 100/400 ft., one target. *Hit:* 9 (1d10 + 2) piercing damage.

Intimidating Shout (Recharge 5-6). The Scavenger releases a fierce battle cry. Each creature of the Scavenger's choice within 30 feet that can hear them must succeed on a DC 13 Wisdom saving throw or be frightened until the end of the Scavenger's next turn.

Description

Scavengers are rugged and muscular individuals, their physiques honed by a harsh life of survival in the decaying city of Lost Angeles. Standing at around 6 feet tall, they wear mismatched pieces of leather armor adorned with scavenged metal plates, providing both protection and a fearsome appearance. Their faces are often obscured by grime and dust, with piercing eyes that constantly scan their surroundings for potential threats or opportunities. Scavengers typically wield scimitars and heavy crossbows, their weapons of choice for close combat and ranged attacks.

Scavengers are a common sight in the deserted streets of Lost Angeles, a once-thriving metropolis now reduced to a decaying ruin. These individuals band together in gangs, patrolling their territories and fiercely defending their resources. The collapse of civilization left them to fend for themselves, and they have adapted to the lawless environment by becoming ruthless and resourceful. Scavengers rely on their physical prowess and tactical acumen to survive, often employing ambush tactics and overwhelming their enemies with sheer numbers.

Life as a Scavenger is brutal and unforgiving, with constant skirmishes over dwindling supplies and safe havens. Despite their rough exterior, some Scavengers hold onto a semblance of loyalty and camaraderie within their gangs, forming bonds that are essential for their survival. Their existence is a testament to the resilience of the human spirit, even when faced with the direst of circumstances. Scavengers embody the harsh reality of life in the Wasteland, where only the strongest and most cunning can hope to endure.

Security Drone

Small construct, unaligned

Armor Class: 14 (natural armor)

Hit Points: 18 (4d6 + 4)

Speed: 0 ft., fly 25 ft. (hover)

STR	DEX	CON	INT	WIS	CHA
8 (-1)	12 (+1)	12 (+1)	8 (-1)	8 (-1)	1 (-5)

Damage Immunities: poison

Condition Immunities: charmed, exhaustion, frightened, poisoned

Senses: darkvision 30 ft., passive Perception 9

Languages: Understands commands in Common but can't speak

Challenge: 1/2 (100 XP)

Actions

Laser Beam: *Ranged Weapon Attack:* +3 to hit, range 40 ft., one target. *Hit:* 5 (1d6 + 1) fire damage.

Taser Shock: *Melee Weapon Attack:* +3 to hit, reach 5 ft., one target. *Hit:* 4 (1d4 + 1) lightning damage and the target must succeed on a DC 11 Constitution saving throw or be stunned until the end of its next turn.

Description

Security Drones are compact, utilitarian constructs designed for basic surveillance and defense. They hover with a slight hum, their boxy frames housing essential sensors and weaponry. These drones feature a basic optical sensor and simple defensive capabilities. While less advanced than their upgraded counterparts, Security Drones still pose a significant threat to intruders in protected areas.

Sun Blight

Medium monstrosity, chaotic evil

Armor Class: 14 (natural armor)

Hit Points: 68 (8d10 + 24)

Speed: 30 ft., fly 40 ft.

STR	DEX	CON	INT	WIS	CHA
16 (+3)	14 (+2)	16 (+3)	6 (-2)	12 (+1)	8 (-1)

Saving Throws: Dex +5, Con +6

Skills: Perception +4, Stealth +5

Damage Resistances: fire

Senses: darkvision 60 ft., passive Perception 14

Languages: --

Challenge: 5 (1,800 XP)

Sunlight Thriving. The Sun Blight has advantage on attack rolls and saving throws while in direct sunlight.

Blinding Carapace. Any creature that starts its turn within 10 feet of the Sun Blight and can see it must succeed on a DC 14 Constitution saving throw or be blinded until the start of its next turn.

Actions

Multiattack. The Sun Blight makes two attacks: one with its bite and one with its claws.

Bite. *Melee Weapon Attack:* +6 to hit, reach 5 ft., one target. *Hit:* 11 (2d6 + 3) piercing damage plus 7 (2d6) fire damage.

Claws. *Melee Weapon Attack:* +6 to hit, reach 5 ft., one target. *Hit:* 8 (1d8 + 3) slashing damage.

Solar Burst (Recharge 5-6). The Sun Blight releases a burst of intense light. Each creature within 20 feet of the Sun Blight that can see it must make a DC 14 Constitution saving throw, taking 21 (6d6) radiant damage on a failed save, or half as much damage on a successful one. A creature that fails the saving throw is also blinded for 1 minute. A blinded creature can repeat the saving throw at the end of each of its turns, ending the effect on itself on a success.

Description

Sun Blights are terrifying insect-like creatures, resembling a nightmarish fusion of a wasp and a beetle. They stand about four feet tall on six spindly legs, their bodies covered in a chitinous exoskeleton that glistens like polished metal under the sun. Their wings are translucent and shimmer with a radiant glow. Sun Blights have multifaceted eyes that reflect the sunlight intensely, and their mandibles are lined with serrated edges, dripping with a fiery venom. Their carapace emits a constant, blinding light that makes direct combat with them dangerous.

Sun Blights are an unnerving product of the Wasteland's extreme conditions, having adapted to thrive in the intense, unrelenting sunlight that scorches the land. These creatures are rarely seen in the shade or darkness, preferring to hunt and move during the peak hours of daylight. Sun Blights often travel in swarms, using their ability to fly to quickly surround and overwhelm their prey. They are notorious for their vicious bite that can cause severe burns, and their radiant bodies can blind those who look directly at them. Legends among the Wasteland survivors tell of entire caravans being wiped out by these relentless predators. The Sun Blights' ability to harness the sun's energy makes them both a fascinating and formidable adversary, embodying the harshness and unpredictability of their environment.

Survivor of Utopia

Medium humanoid (human), neutral good

Armor Class: 14 (leather armor)

Hit Points: 45 (6d8 + 18)

Speed: 30 ft.

STR	DEX	CON	INT	WIS	CHA
14 (+2)	16 (+3)	16 (+3)	12 (+1)	14 (+2)	10 (+0)

Saving Throws: Dex +5, Con +5

Skills: Perception +4, Stealth +5, Survival +6, Medicine +4

Senses: passive Perception 14

Languages: Common, Elvish

Challenge: 2 (450 XP)

Resourceful Survivor. The Survivor of Utopia has advantage on Wisdom (Survival) checks made to find food, water, or shelter.

Resilient. The Survivor has advantage on saving throws against being poisoned and has resistance to poison damage.

Actions

Multiattack. The Survivor makes two melee attacks.

Shortsword. *Melee Weapon Attack:* +5 to hit, reach 5 ft., one target. *Hit:* 7 (1d6 + 3) piercing damage.

Shortbow. *Ranged Weapon Attack:* +5 to hit, range 80/320 ft., one target. *Hit:* 7 (1d6 + 3) piercing damage.

First Aid (3/Day). The Survivor can use their action to administer first aid to a creature within 5 feet. The target regains 10 hit points.

Tactical Retreat. As a bonus action, the Survivor can disengage or dash.

Second Wind (Recharges after a Short or Long Rest). The Survivor can use a bonus action to regain 1d10 + 6 hit points.

Description

The Survivor of Utopia is a rugged, wiry individual with sun-kissed skin and a lean, muscular build honed by the harsh conditions of the Wasteland. They wear a patchwork of leather armor and scavenged materials, providing both protection and mobility. Their eyes are sharp and alert, constantly scanning their surroundings for potential threats or opportunities. A short sword hangs at their side, and a shortbow is slung over their back, along with a quiver of arrows. The Survivor's appearance is both practical and battle-worn, marked by scars and signs of countless close encounters with danger.

Survivors of Utopia are the hardened remnants of a once-thriving community now struggling to endure in the post-apocalyptic world. These individuals have adapted to the harsh realities of the Wasteland through sheer determination and resourcefulness. They are skilled hunters and gatherers, capable of finding sustenance where others see only desolation. Known for their resilience, Survivors are adept at treating wounds and illnesses, often serving as medics and caretakers within their enclaves. Despite the relentless challenges they face, Survivors of Utopia maintain a strong sense of community and hope, driven by the belief that they can rebuild and thrive once more. They are often found on the front lines of exploration and defense, embodying the spirit of endurance and adaptability that defines their people.

Swarmers

Medium swarm of Tiny beasts, unaligned

Armor Class: 13

Hit Points: 75 (10d8 + 30)

Speed: 30 ft., fly 30 ft.

STR	DEX	CON	INT	WIS	CHA
8 (-1)	16 (+3)	16 (+3)	3 (-4)	12 (+1)	6 (-2)

Damage Resistances: bludgeoning, piercing, slashing

Condition Immunities: charmed, frightened, grappled, paralyzed, petrified, prone, restrained, stunned

Senses: darkvision 60 ft., passive Perception 11

Languages: --

Challenge: 5 (1,800 XP)

Swarm. The swarm can occupy another creature's space and vice versa, and the swarm can move through any opening large enough for a Tiny insect. The swarm can't regain hit points or gain temporary hit points.

Overwhelm. The swarm has advantage on attack rolls against a creature whose space it occupies.

Actions

Multiattack. The swarm makes two Swarm Bite attacks.

Swarm Bite. *Melee Weapon Attack:* +6 to hit, reach 0 ft., one target in the swarm's space. *Hit:* 21 (6d6)

piercing damage, or 10 (3d6) piercing damage if the swarm has half of its hit points or fewer.

Devour (Recharge 5-6). The Swarmers unleash a concentrated assault on a creature within their space. The target must make a DC 15 Constitution saving throw, taking 28 (8d6) piercing damage on a failed save, or half as much damage on a successful one. If the target is reduced to 0 hit points by this damage, it is devoured and the swarm regains 20 hit points.

Description

Swarmers are a terrifying mass of small, mutated insects that move as a single, writhing entity. Individually, they are about the size of a large beetle, with hardened, segmented exoskeletons and numerous spiny legs. Their eyes glow with an unnatural, malevolent light, and their mandibles are razor-sharp, capable of slicing through flesh with ease. When they swarm, they create a cacophony of buzzing and chittering that can be heard from a distance, a prelude to the horror they bring.

Swarmers are a product of the Wasteland's harsh environment and rampant mutation, originally benign insects now twisted into voracious predators. These creatures have developed a hive mind, allowing them to act in perfect unison, coordinating their attacks with lethal efficiency. They swarm over their prey, overwhelming and devouring creatures much larger than themselves within moments. The origins of these mutated insects are a topic of much speculation among survivors. Some believe they are the result of exposure to toxic waste or radiation, while others think they might have been part of a failed biological experiment. Whatever their origin, Swarmers are a dire threat to any living being they encounter. Their relentless hunger and ability to rapidly reproduce make them one of the most feared entities in the Wasteland, capable of reducing even the hardiest of creatures to bones in a matter of minutes.

Techno-Ghost

Medium undead (incorporeal), chaotic neutral

Armor Class: 13

Hit Points: 67 (9d8 + 27)

Speed: 0 ft., fly 40 ft. (hover)

STR	DEX	CON	INT	WIS	CHA
8 (-1)	16 (+3)	16 (+3)	14 (+2)	12 (+1)	18 (+4)

Damage Resistances: cold, lightning, necrotic; bludgeoning, piercing, and slashing from nonmagical attacks

Damage Immunities: aoison

Condition Immunities: charmed, exhaustion, grappled, paralyzed, petrified, poisoned, prone, restrained

Senses: darkvision 60 ft., passive Perception 11

Languages: Common, Binary (understands but cannot speak)

Challenge: 6 (2,300 XP)

Ethereal Sight. The Techno-Ghost can see 60 feet into the Ethereal Plane when it is on the Material Plane, and vice versa.

Incorporeal Movement. The Techno-Ghost can move through other creatures and objects as if they were difficult terrain. It takes 5 (1d10) force damage if it ends its turn inside an object.

Actions

Multiattack. The Techno-Ghost makes two Shock Touch attacks.

Shock Touch. *Melee Spell Attack:* +7 to hit, reach 5 ft., one target. *Hit:* 17 (4d6 + 3) lightning damage.

Electromagnetic Pulse (Recharge 5-6). The Techno-Ghost emits a pulse of electromagnetic energy. Each creature within a 20-foot radius must make a DC 15 Constitution saving throw, taking 27 (6d8) lightning damage on a failed save, or half as much damage on a successful one. Constructs and creatures with electronic components have disadvantage on the saving throw and are stunned for 1 minute on a failed save. A stunned creature can repeat the saving throw at the end of each of its turns, ending the effect on itself on a success.

Description

Techno-Ghosts are eerie, translucent apparitions that flicker and distort like a hologram experiencing interference. Their forms vaguely resemble humanoid figures clad in the remnants of old-world security uniforms, with features obscured by digital static. Faint, glowing circuitry patterns trace across their spectral bodies, illuminating the air with a cold, blue light. Their eyes, if they can be called that, are hollow voids that pulse with an unsettling energy. These entities drift silently through their environments, their presence marked by a faint hum of electronic interference.

Techno-Ghosts are the spectral remnants of advanced security systems from the old world, twisted into a semblance of life by the catastrophic events that ravaged the land. When the Catastrophe struck, many of these systems were left in ruins, their AI components corrupted and fragmented. Over time, these digital echoes coalesced into ghostly forms, driven by fragmented protocols and a haunting semblance of purpose. They inhabit the ruins of once-secure facilities, phasing through walls and monitoring the remnants of their domains.

Techno-Ghosts are known to disrupt electronic devices and constructs with their electromagnetic pulses, a vestige of their original function to secure and control. Survivors who encounter these beings often describe the experience as unnerving, with the Techno-Ghosts' erratic behavior and chilling presence leaving a lasting impression. Some believe that these entities are seeking to fulfill long-forgotten directives, while others view them as mere anomalies, byproducts of the technological advancements that ultimately led to society's downfall. Regardless of their true nature, Techno-Ghosts are a stark reminder of the old world's lost grandeur and the lingering consequences of its collapse.

Toxic Sludge

Large ooze, unaligned

Armor Class: 8

Hit Points: 105 (10d10 + 50)

Speed: 20 ft., climb 20 ft.

STR	DEX	CON	INT	WIS	CHA
18 (+4)	6 (-2)	20 (+5)	1 (-5)	6 (-2)	1 (-5)

Damage Resistances: acid, poison

Damage Immunities: bludgeoning, piercing, and slashing from nonmagical attacks

Condition Immunities: blinded, charmed, deafened, exhaustion, frightened, prone

Senses: blindsight 60 ft. (blind beyond this radius), passive Perception 8

Languages: --

Challenge: 7 (2,900 XP)

Amorphous. The sludge can move through a space as narrow as 1 inch wide without squeezing.

Corrosive Form. A creature that touches the sludge or hits it with a melee attack while within 5 feet of it takes 10 (3d6) acid damage.

Engulf. The sludge moves up to its speed. While doing so, it can enter Large or smaller creatures' spaces. Whenever the sludge enters a creature's space, the creature must make a DC 15 Dexterity saving throw. On a successful save, the creature can choose to be pushed 5 feet back or to the side of the sludge. A creature that chooses not to be pushed suffers the consequences of a failed saving throw. On a failed save, the sludge enters the creature's space, and the creature takes 21 (6d6) acid damage and is engulfed. The engulfed creature can't breathe, is restrained, and takes 21 (6d6) acid damage at the start of each of the sludge's turns. When the sludge moves, the engulfed creature moves with it. An engulfed creature can try to escape by taking an action to make a DC 15 Strength check. On a success, the creature escapes and enters a space of its choice within 5 feet of the sludge.

Actions

Multiattack. The sludge makes two Pseudopod attacks.

Pseudopod. *Melee Weapon Attack:* +7 to hit, reach 10 ft., one target. *Hit:* 14 (2d8 + 4) acid damage.

Description

The Toxic Sludge appears as a large, amorphous blob of dark, iridescent green ooze, pulsating and bubbling with the foul stench of decay. Its surface constantly shifts and churns, with tendrils of viscous liquid extending and retracting seemingly at random. Within its semi-transparent form, the remains of organic and inorganic matter can sometimes be seen, slowly dissolving into the sludge. The creature moves with a sluggish, yet purposeful, flow, leaving a trail of corrosive residue in its wake.

Toxic Sludges are a byproduct of the environmental devastation that plagues the Wasteland. Formed from concentrated pools of industrial waste and toxic runoff, these amorphous blobs have inexplicably gained a semblance of life. Driven by an instinctual need to consume and dissolve any material they come into contact with, Toxic Sludges pose a significant threat to any living beings or structures they encounter. Their corrosive nature allows them to break down nearly any substance, absorbing it into their ever-growing mass. Legends among Wasteland survivors speak of entire settlements being overrun by these relentless oozes, their inhabitants dissolved into nothingness. Despite their dangerous nature, some brave (or foolish) individuals seek out Toxic Sludges, hoping to harvest their corrosive essence for use in crafting powerful acids or potent toxins. However, few who attempt this hazardous task return unscathed, if at all.

Wasteland Raider

Medium humanoid (human), chaotic evil

Armor Class: 15 (studded leather armor)

Hit Points: 52 (8d8 + 16)

Speed: 30 ft.

STR	DEX	CON	INT	WIS	CHA
14 (+2)	16 (+3)	14 (+2)	10 (+0)	11 (+0)	12 (+1)

Saving Throws: Dex +5, Con +4

Skills: Athletics +4, Intimidation +5, Perception +4, Stealth +5

Senses: passive Perception 14

Languages: Common, Goblin

Challenge: 3 (700 XP)

Pack Tactics. The raider has advantage on an attack roll against a creature if at least one of the raider's allies is within 5 feet of the creature and the ally isn't incapacitated.

Savage Tactics. The raider can use a bonus action to take the Dash or Disengage action.

Actions

Multiattack. The raider makes two melee attacks or two ranged attacks.

Scimitar. *Melee Weapon Attack:* +5 to hit, reach 5 ft., one target. *Hit:* 7 (1d6 + 3) slashing damage.

Light Crossbow. *Ranged Weapon Attack:* +5 to hit, range 80/320 ft., one target. *Hit:* 8 (1d8 + 3) piercing damage.

Reckless Charge (1/Day). The raider can move up to their speed toward a hostile creature that they can see. They can then make one melee attack with advantage. Until the start of the raider's next turn, attack rolls against them have advantage.

Legendary Actions

The raider can take 1 legendary action per round, choosing from the options below. Only one legendary action option can be used at a time and only at the end of another creature's turn. The raider regains spent legendary actions at the start of its turn.

Intimidating Shout. The raider targets one creature within 30 feet. The target must succeed on a DC 13 Wisdom saving throw or be frightened until the end of the raider's next turn.

Description

Wasteland Raiders are a ragtag and fearsome sight, embodying the desperation and brutality of the post-apocalyptic world. Clad in mismatched pieces of scavenged armor, they wear studded leather patched with metal plates, giving them a rugged and intimidating appearance. Their faces are often obscured by makeshift masks or bandanas, with eyes that gleam with malice and opportunism. Raiders are heavily armed with an assortment of weapons ranging from scimitars and daggers to crossbows and salvaged firearms. Their bodies are lean and muscular, honed by a life of constant conflict and survival.

Wasteland Raiders are bands of human Scavengers who have turned to marauding as a means of survival in the harsh and resource-scarce environment. Originally ordinary survivors, the relentless struggle for food, water, and shelter has driven them to ruthless extremes. They roam the Wasteland in groups, preying on weaker settlements and travelers, using their superior numbers and tactics to overwhelm their victims. Raiders operate with a code of brutal efficiency, taking what they need by force and leaving destruction in their wake. Their leaders are often the most cunning and ruthless among them, maintaining control through fear and the promise of spoils. Despite their savagery, Raiders are not mindless; they are capable of strategic planning and have an acute awareness of the terrain and the weaknesses of their targets. Their existence is a grim reminder of the lengths to which humanity can be driven in the fight for survival.

NPC

NPCs

Commander Rylan

Medium humanoid (human), lawful neutral

Armor Class: 18 (plate armor)

Hit Points: 136 (16d8 + 64)

Speed: 30 ft.

STR	DEX	CON	INT	WIS	CHA
18 (+4)	12 (+1)	18 (+4)	14 (+2)	16 (+3)	14 (+2)

Saving Throws: Str +8, Con +8, Wis +7

Skills: Athletics +8, Intimidation +6, Perception +7, Survival +7

Senses: passive Perception 17

Languages: Common

Challenge: 8 (3,900 XP)

Actions

Multiattack. Commander Rylan makes three melee attacks.

Longsword. *Melee Weapon Attack:* +8 to hit, reach 5 ft., one target. *Hit:* 11 (1d10 + 4) slashing damage.

Hand Crossbow. *Ranged Weapon Attack:* +5 to hit, range 30/120 ft., one target. *Hit:* 7 (1d6 + 1) piercing damage.

Tactical Leadership (Recharge 5-6). Commander Rylan can use a bonus action to grant all allies within 30 feet advantage on their next attack roll before the start of his next turn.

Indomitable (3/Day). Commander Rylan can reroll a saving throw that he fails. He must use the new roll.

Second Wind (1/Day). As a bonus action, Commander Rylan can regain 20 hit points.

Battlefield Presence. Allies within 10 feet of Commander Rylan gain a +2 bonus to AC and saving throws while they can see and hear him.

Legendary Actions

Commander Rylan can take 3 legendary actions, choosing from the options below. Only one legendary action option can be used at a time and only at the end of another creature's turn. Commander Rylan regains spent legendary actions at the start of his turn.

Command Ally. Commander Rylan targets one ally he can see within 30 feet of him. If the target can see and hear him, the target can immediately make one weapon attack as a reaction.

Reposition (Costs 2 Actions). Commander Rylan can move up to his speed without provoking opportunity attacks.

Rallying Cry (Costs 3 Actions). Commander Rylan and all allies within 30 feet of him regain 10 hit points.

Description

Commander Rylan is a formidable figure, standing at an imposing six feet tall with a muscular build honed from years of rigorous military training. His steel-grey hair is cropped short, and his stern, weathered face is marked with scars that tell of countless battles. Rylan's piercing blue eyes reflect a sharp intellect and unwavering determination. He wears meticulously maintained plate armor adorned with the insignia of the Preservation, exuding an aura of authority and command.

Commander Rylan's journey to leadership was forged in the fires of adversity and loss. Rylan survives the post-Catastrophe world and its ensuing chaos by sheer will and tactical brilliance. His pragmatic and often ruthless decisions have saved countless lives, but they have also earned him a reputation for being unyielding and cold. Driven by a deep sense of duty to protect what remains of civilization, Rylan's greatest fault is his inability to trust others fully, often bearing the weight of leadership alone. His rigid adherence to rules and his belief in the necessity of strict order can sometimes blind him to more compassionate solutions. Despite his stern exterior,

Rylan is haunted by the memory of his family, lost in the early days of the disaster, and he channels his grief into an unrelenting commitment to his mission.

Elder Maren

Medium humanoid (human), lawful neutral

Armor Class: 15 (natural armor)

Hit Points: 88 (13d8 + 26)

Speed: 30 ft.

STR	DEX	CON	INT	WIS	CHA
10 (+0)	12 (+1)	14 (+2)	18 (+4)	20 (+5)	16 (+3)

Saving Throws: Int +8, Wis +9, Cha +7

Skills: Insight +9, Medicine +9, History +8, Persuasion +7

Senses: passive Perception 15

Languages: Common, Elvish, Dwarvish

Challenge: 7 (2,900 XP)

Actions

Multiattack. Maren makes two melee attacks or two ranged attacks.

Quarterstaff. *Melee Weapon Attack:* +4 to hit, reach 5 ft., one target. *Hit:* 6 (1d8 + 2) bludgeoning damage.

Guiding Bolt. *Ranged Spell Attack:* +9 to hit, range 120 ft., one target. *Hit:* 20 (4d6) radiant damage, and the next attack roll made against this target before the end of Maren's next turn has advantage.

Spellcasting. Maren is a 9th-level spellcaster. Her spellcasting ability is Wisdom (spell save DC 17, +9 to hit with spell attacks). She has the following cleric spells prepared:

- Cantrips (at will): *Guidance, Light, Sacred Flame, Spare the Dying*
- 1st level (4 slots): *Bless, Command, Cure Wounds, Sanctuary*
- 2nd level (3 slots): *Hold Person, Lesser Restoration, Spiritual Weapon*
- 3rd level (3 slots): *Dispel Magic, Revivify, Spirit Guardians*
- 4th level (3 slots): *Banishment, Death Ward, Guardian of Faith*
- 5th level (1 slot): *Mass Cure Wounds*

Healing Touch (3/Day). Maren touches another creature and restores 30 hit points to it.

Aura of Wisdom. Allies within 10 feet of Maren gain a +2 bonus to Wisdom saving throws.

Legendary Actions

Maren can take 2 legendary actions, choosing from the options below. Only one legendary action option can be used at a time and only at the end of another creature's turn. Maren regains spent legendary actions at the start of her turn.

Healing Word. Maren casts *Healing Word* at 1st level.

Insightful Command. Maren grants an ally within 30 feet advantage on their next attack roll or ability check.

Description

Elder Maren is a dignified woman in her sixties, standing at about 5'6" with a graceful bearing that commands respect. Her long, silver hair flows freely down her back, and her piercing green eyes reflect both wisdom and a lifetime of experience. Her weathered face is marked with fine lines, each telling a story of the many challenges she has faced. Maren dresses in flowing robes adorned with symbols of her hidden society, and she carries a simple, yet elegant quarterstaff. Her demeanor is calm and measured, exuding an air of serenity and authority.

Elder Maren's journey to leadership was shaped by her insatiable thirst for knowledge and an unwavering commitment to her people. Born into a prominent family within Hope Fall's society, she was groomed from a young age to understand the intricacies of their way of life and the vital importance of the water source they guarded. Her exceptional intellect and keen insight quickly set her apart, and she rose through the ranks to become the society's leader. Maren is driven by a profound sense of duty to protect her people and the precious water source they rely on. Her cautious nature stems from years of witnessing the devastating consequences of careless actions and betrayal.

However, Maren's caution can sometimes verge on paranoia, leading her to be overly suspicious of outsiders and even members of her own society. Her reluctance to take risks often causes friction with those who believe in more aggressive or innovative approaches. Despite her wisdom, Maren is haunted by the fear of failing her people and the legacy of her ancestors. This fear drives her to make calculated decisions that prioritize the long-term survival of the society over immediate gains. Elder Maren's complex character is a blend of wisdom, caution, and an unyielding commitment to her people, making her a pivotal figure in the quest for survival beyond the Wall.

Engineer Liora

Medium humanoid (human), lawful neutral

Armor Class: 14 (studded leather armor)

Hit Points: 76 (9d8 + 36)

Speed: 30 ft.

STR	DEX	CON	INT	WIS	CHA
12 (+1)	16 (+3)	18 (+4)	20 (+5)	14 (+2)	10 (+0)

Saving Throws: Dex +6, Int +8, Wis +5

Skills: Investigation +8, Perception +5, Arcana +8, History +8

Senses: passive Perception 15

Languages: Common, Dwarvish, Elvish

Challenge: 6 (2,300 XP)

Defensive Tactics. Allies within 10 feet of Liora gain a +1 bonus to AC while they can see and hear her.

Gadgeteer (1/Day). Liora can deploy a mechanical gadget of her design. Choose one of the following effects:

- **Flashbang:** Creatures within a 15-foot radius must succeed on a DC 15 Constitution saving throw or be blinded and deafened for 1 minute.

- **Repair Drone:** A small drone repairs an ally, healing 20 hit points.

Actions

Multiattack. Liora makes two melee attacks.

Wrench. *Melee Weapon Attack:* +6 to hit, reach 5 ft., one target. *Hit:* 8 (1d8 + 3) bludgeoning damage.

Hand Crossbow. *Ranged Weapon Attack:* +6 to hit, range 30/120 ft., one target. *Hit:* 7 (1d6 + 3) piercing damage.

Technical Expertise (Recharge 5-6). Liora can use her action to analyze a mechanical or magical device within 30 feet, identifying its purpose and how to operate or disable it.

Field Repairs. Liora can use her action to repair a damaged object or construct within 5 feet. The object or construct regains 20 hit points.

Legendary Actions

Liora can take 2 legendary actions, choosing from the options below. Only one legendary action option can be used at a time and only at the end of another creature's turn. Liora regains spent legendary actions at the start of her turn.

Analyze Weakness. Liora targets one creature she can see within 30 feet. The next attack made against that creature before the start of her next turn has advantage.

Reinforce (Costs 2 Actions). Liora can provide a temporary boost to an ally's defenses. That ally gains a +2 bonus to AC until the start of Liora's next turn.

Description

Engineer Liora is a woman in her early forties with an athletic build, standing at around 5'8". She has a mass of curly auburn hair usually tied back in a practical bun to keep it out of her intense, intelligent hazel eyes. Her face, often smudged with grease and soot, is marked by a determined expression and the faint lines of stress and concentration. Liora wears studded leather armor customized with numerous pockets and straps holding various tools and gadgets essential for her work. Her hands are calloused and skilled, always ready to repair or analyze a piece of machinery.

Engineer Liora was born into a family of renowned engineers and inventors, inheriting a legacy of brilliance and innovation. From a young age, she showed exceptional talent in understanding and creating complex mechanical systems. Her intellectual prowess earned her a prominent position overseeing the Wall's maintenance, a role she takes immense pride in. Driven by a relentless pursuit of perfection and a desire to uphold her family's legacy, Liora is committed to maintaining the Wall and ensuring the safety of her community. However, her dedication to her work often comes at a personal cost. She struggles with perfectionism and tends to be overly critical of herself and others. This has led to strained relationships with her peers, as she can be perceived as aloof and uncompromising. Despite her flaws, her expertise and unwavering commitment make her an indispensable asset to the Preservation and the survival of Utopia.

Pipemaster Jax

Medium humanoid (human), chaotic neutral

Armor Class: 13 (improvised armor)

Hit Points: 92 (12d8 + 36)

Speed: 30 ft.

STR	DEX	CON	INT	WIS	CHA
12 (+1)	14 (+2)	16 (+3)	18 (+4)	12 (+1)	10 (+0)

Saving Throws: Dex +5, Int +7, Con +6

Skills: Investigation +7, Perception +4, Sleight of Hand +5, Survival +4

Senses: darkvision 60 ft., passive Perception 14

Languages: Common, Dwarvish, Gnomish

Challenge: 5 (1,800 XP)

Resourceful Tactician. Jax can use the Help action as a bonus action, and when he does, the ally he helps also gains a +1 bonus to their AC until the start of Jax's next turn.

Actions

Multiattack. Jax makes two melee attacks.

Wrench. *Melee Weapon Attack:* +5 to hit, reach 5 ft., one target. *Hit:* 9 (2d6 + 2) bludgeoning damage.

Improvised Crossbow. *Ranged Weapon Attack:* +5 to hit, range 30/120 ft., one target. *Hit:* 7 (1d8 + 2) piercing damage.

Mechanical Savvy (Recharge 5-6). Jax can use his action to disable a mechanical trap or device within 30 feet. Alternatively, he can give advantage to an ally's next Intelligence check to operate a device.

Improvised Explosives. Jax can throw a homemade explosive within 60 feet. Each creature in a 10-foot radius must make a DC 15 Dexterity saving throw, taking 21 (6d6) fire damage on a failed save, or half as much damage on a successful one.

Legendary Actions

Jax can take 2 legendary actions, choosing from the options below. Only one legendary action option can be used at a time and only at the end of another creature's turn. Jax regains spent legendary actions at the start of his turn.

Quick Fix. Jax uses his Mechanical Savvy to repair a damaged object or device within 5 feet, restoring 10 hit points to it.

Evasive Maneuver (Costs 2 Actions). Jax moves up to his speed without provoking opportunity attacks.

Description

Pipemaster Jax is a wiry man in his late forties, with a lean build that speaks to years of navigating tight, confined spaces. His hair is a wild tangle of dark curls streaked with gray, and his face is perpetually smeared with grime and oil. Jax's eyes are a piercing blue, always darting around as if assessing his surroundings for the next potential hazard or opportunity. He wears a patchwork of leather and metal armor, cobbled together from various scraps he has scavenged, with numerous pockets and tool belts hanging from his waist.

Jax was once a celebrated engineer, known for his ingenious designs and unconventional methods. When a rival faction attacked his home, he lost everything: his family, his career, and the world he knew. Driven by a desperate need to survive and a refusal to let his skills go to waste, Jax took to the pipelines, making them his new home. His intimate knowledge of the infrastructure became his lifeline. Jax is driven by a fierce independence and a desire to stay one step ahead of the chaos that claimed his past. However, his solitary life has made him paranoid and distrustful, often pushing away those who try to get close. He harbors a deep resentment for authority figures, blaming them for the downfall of civilization, and this makes him a reluctant

ally at best. Despite his flaws, Jax's expertise and resourcefulness make him an invaluable guide through the treacherous pipelines, even if his motives are not always entirely selfless.

Quartermaster Tags

Medium humanoid (human), neutral good

Armor Class: 15 (leather armor)

Hit Points: 85 (10d8 + 40)

Speed: 30 ft.

STR	DEX	CON	INT	WIS	CHA
10 (+0)	16 (+3)	18 (+4)	14 (+2)	15 (+2)	13 (+1)

Saving Throws: Dex +6, Con +7, Wis +5

Skills: Insight +5, Perception +5, Persuasion +4, Investigation +5

Senses: passive Perception 15

Languages: Common

Challenge: 5 (1,800 XP)

Supply Drop (1/Day). Tags can produce a set of adventuring gear or healing supplies (up to 50 gp value) from her pack to assist her allies.

Supportive Command. Allies within 10 feet of Tags gain a +1 bonus to AC and saving throws while they can see and hear her.

Quick Thinking. Tags can take the Dash, Disengage, or Help action as a bonus action.

Actions

Multiattack. Tags makes two ranged attacks.

Hand Crossbow. *Ranged Weapon Attack:* +6 to hit, range 30/120 ft., one target. *Hit:* 8 (1d6 + 3) piercing damage.

Dagger. *Melee Weapon Attack:* +6 to hit, reach 5 ft., one target. *Hit:* 6 (1d4 + 3) piercing damage.

Resourceful Tactician (Recharge 5-6). Tags can use a bonus action to allow an ally within 30 feet to reroll one failed saving throw or attack roll.

Legendary Actions

Tags can take 2 legendary actions, choosing from the options below. Only one legendary action option can be used at a time and only at the end of another creature's turn. Tags regains spent legendary actions at the start of her turn.

Coordinate. Tags targets one ally she can see within 30 feet of her. That ally can immediately move up to half its speed without provoking opportunity attacks.

Replenish (Costs 2 Actions). Tags provides an ally within 5 feet with a healing potion, allowing them to regain 10 hit points.

Description

Quartermaster Tags is a lithe and agile woman in her mid-thirties, standing at about 5'7". She has short, curly brown hair that is often tied back, and sharp green eyes that seem to take in everything around her. Her tan skin is dotted with freckles, and she has a calm, composed demeanor. Tags typically wears practical leather armor adorned with various pouches and packs filled with supplies, tools, and small weapons. Her hands are always busy, either organizing gear or taking inventory.

Tags grew up in the chaotic aftermath of the Catastrophe, learning from an early age the value of resourcefulness and quick thinking. Orphaned during a raid on her small community, she was taken in by a group of wandering traders who taught her the art of negotiation, bartering, and survival. Driven by a deep-seated need to ensure others don't suffer as she did, Tags dedicated herself to becoming a master of supply and logistics. She is known for her keen intellect and ability to make scarce resources stretch further than anyone thought possible. However, her relentless drive to maintain order and provide for her community often leads her to overextend herself, taking on too much responsibility and neglecting her own well-being. Tags's fear of failure and letting others down can sometimes cause her to be overly controlling and distrustful, pushing her to micromanage even when she should delegate. Despite these flaws, her heart is in the right place, and she is unwaveringly loyal to those she cares about.

Scavenger Leader Kael

Medium humanoid (human), chaotic evil

Armor Class: 17 (patchwork armor)

Hit Points: 112 (15d8 + 45)

Speed: 30 ft.

STR	DEX	CON	INT	WIS	CHA
18 (+4)	14 (+2)	16 (+3)	12 (+1)	10 (+0)	14 (+2)

Saving Throws: Str +7, Con +6, Wis +3

Skills: Intimidation +7, Athletics +7, Survival +6

Senses: passive Perception 10

Languages: Common, Goblin

Challenge: 8 (3,900 XP)

Intimidating Presence. Kael can use his bonus action to impose disadvantage on attack rolls against him from a creature he can see within 30 feet until the end of his next turn.

Savage Strike (1/Day). Kael can make a single melee attack with advantage. If the attack hits, it deals an extra 14 (4d6) damage.

Actions

Multiattack. Kael makes three melee attacks.

Greatsword. *Melee Weapon Attack:* +7 to hit, reach 5 ft., one target. *Hit:* 12 (2d6 + 4) slashing damage.

Heavy Crossbow. *Ranged Weapon Attack:* +5 to hit, range 100/400 ft., one target. *Hit:* 9 (1d10 + 4) piercing damage.

Brutal Leadership (Recharge 5-6). Kael can use his action to issue a command that frightens his enemies. All creatures of his choice within 30 feet must succeed on a DC 15 Wisdom saving throw or be frightened for 1 minute. A frightened target can repeat the saving throw at the end of each of its turns, ending the effect on itself on a success.

Legendary Actions

Kael can take 2 legendary actions, choosing from the options below. Only one legendary action option can be used at a time and only at the end of another creature's turn. Kael regains spent legendary actions at the start of his turn.

Command Ally. Kael targets one ally he can see within 30 feet. If the target can see and hear him, the target can immediately make one weapon attack as a reaction.

Reposition (Costs 2 Actions). Kael can move up to his speed without provoking opportunity attacks.

Description

Scavenger Leader Kael is a hulking figure, standing at 6'4" with a broad, muscular build that has been hardened by the harsh conditions of Lost Angeles. His skin is deeply tanned and weathered from prolonged exposure to the scorching sun. Kael's eyes are a wild, piercing blue, often glinting with a dangerous mix of cunning and madness. His head is shaved, revealing a series of scars that mark past battles. Kael's armor is a patchwork of scavenged materials, providing both protection and a display of his ruthless efficiency. He carries a greatsword slung across his back, and his hands are never far from the hilt.

Kael's descent into brutality began long before he took control of his Scavenger faction. Once a skilled mechanic, Kael's mind began to fray under the relentless sun and the ceaseless threats of the Wasteland. As resources dwindled and sanity became a luxury, Kael's natural leadership qualities twisted into something darker. He seized power through fear and violence, eliminating anyone who challenged his authority with ruthless efficiency. Kael's need for control is driven by a deep-seated fear of vulnerability and chaos, a fear that often manifests as extreme paranoia and a hair-trigger temper. His mind, addled by the heat and the insanity of Lost Angeles, oscillates between moments of strategic brilliance and uncontrollable rage. Despite his brutality, Kael possesses a shrewd understanding of survival, knowing when to offer aid or strike deals if it benefits his position. His leadership is marked by a delicate balance of fear and grudging respect from his followers, who know that defiance could mean death. Kael's complex character is a blend of fear-driven tyranny and the desperate need to maintain his crumbling empire in the heart of a dying city.

Skywatcher Finn

Medium humanoid (human), chaotic good

Armor Class: 16 (studded leather armor)

Hit Points: 85 (10d8 + 40)

Speed: 35 ft.

STR	DEX	CON	INT	WIS	CHA
14 (+2)	18 (+4)	18 (+4)	12 (+1)	16 (+3)	14 (+2)

Saving Throws: Dex +7, Con +7, Wis +6

Skills: Perception +9, Stealth +7, Survival +6, Insight +6

Senses: passive Perception 19

Languages: Common, Elvish, Thieves' Cant

Challenge: 6 (2,300 XP)

Scout's Agility. Finn can take the Dash, Disengage, or Hide action as a bonus action on each of his turns.

Actions

Multiattack. Finn makes two ranged attacks.

Longbow. *Ranged Weapon Attack:* +7 to hit, range 150/600 ft., one target. *Hit:* 9 (1d8 + 4) piercing damage.

Shortsword. *Melee Weapon Attack:* +7 to hit, reach 5 ft., one target. *Hit:* 8 (1d6 + 4) slashing damage.

Eagle Eye (Recharge 5-6). Finn can use his bonus action to grant himself advantage on all ranged attack rolls until the end of his turn.

Quirky Humor. Finn can use his action to taunt a creature within 30 feet. The target must succeed on a DC 15 Wisdom saving throw or have disadvantage on attack rolls against Finn until the end of its next turn.

Legendary Actions

Finn can take 2 legendary actions, choosing from the options below. Only one legendary action option can be used at a time and only at the end of another creature's turn. Finn regains spent legendary actions at the start of his turn.

Swift Shot. Finn makes a ranged attack with his longbow.

Evasive Maneuver. Finn moves up to his speed without provoking opportunity attacks.

Description

Skywatcher Finn is a lean, wiry man in his late thirties, standing at about 5'11". His hair is a tousled mop of sandy blond, and his sharp green eyes constantly scan the horizon with an intensity born of years spent in vigilance. His face is often lit up with a mischievous grin, hinting at his quirky sense of humor. Finn's attire consists of well-worn, dark green studded leather armor that blends seamlessly with his surroundings, adorned with various pockets and pouches for his scouting tools. He moves with the lithe grace of someone who has spent countless hours navigating treacherous terrain.

Finn's early life was marked by tragedy and loss, having been orphaned at a young age by the chaos of the Wasteland. Taken in by a group of nomadic survivors, he learned the skills of a scout and tracker, finding solace in the solitude of the wilderness. His sharp wit and quick reflexes made him an invaluable asset, but his penchant for humor often put him at odds with more serious members of the group. Driven by a desire to understand the land and its secrets, Finn eventually made his way to the Wall, where he found a perch that offered a perfect vantage point for his observations.

Despite his outwardly jovial demeanor, Finn is deeply haunted by the loss of his family and the countless hardships he has endured. His humor serves as a defense mechanism, keeping others at a distance and masking the pain he carries. Finn's reluctance to form close bonds stems from a fear of losing those he cares about, leading him to a life of reclusion. However, his innate curiosity and sense of duty compel him to assist those who seek his knowledge. Finn's complex personality and invaluable expertise make him a unique and memorable character in the world beyond the Wall.

Maps

Maps

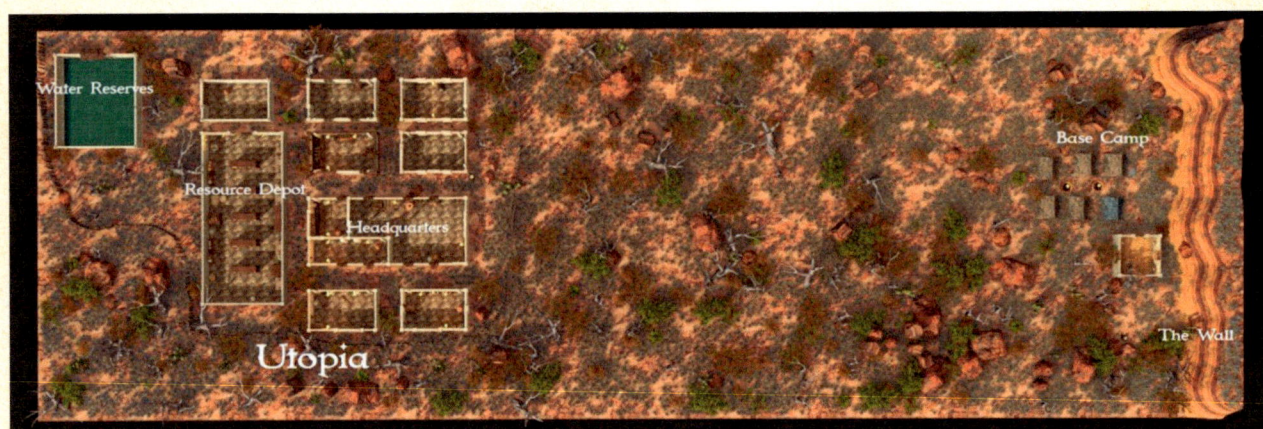

Act 1

Act 3

Thank You

Thank You

AbdulAziz Al-Kaboor

Billy and Niki Jones

Buddha Weatherby

Brian Schapp

C. B. Pelton

Cameron Zipf

David Stephenson

For E.K. Hudson and all who battle P.T.S.D.

Ironcrown

Isaac Wurmbrand

Jake and Jack Ramirez

Jason Taylor

Jayson Holovacs

Jon Newlands

Karl Reichle

Laura Rassier

Lunara Lilith

Melissa Iverson

Michael G Palmer

Michelle McFarlin

Mike Trisevic

Ragemaw

Rowan Stone

Paul Hebert

Shawn Cascy

Wes Painter